A Song in the Desert

A Song in the Desert

R M WILLIAMS

Angus&Robertson
An imprint of HarperCollins*Publishers*

Angus&Robertson

An imprint of HarperCollins*Publishers*, Australia

First published in Australia in 1998
by HarperCollins*Publishers* Pty Limited
ACN 009 913 517
A member of the HarperCollins*Publishers* (Australia) Pty Limited Group
http://www.harpercollins.com.au

Photographs from the author's private collection
Page vi: Wade (l) and author; chapter opener pages: R.M. Williams, aged 24;
p. 18: Just like home; p. 19: A 'ship of the desert'; p. 28: Rock hole water;
p. 32: Wade bathing a woman with yaws; p. 39: Child dancing; p. 49: Running
creek, 'Ernabella'; p. 62: Youths after a hunt; p. 83: Hobbled camel;
p. 92: A team of camels at work; p 128: Wade with desert tribe; p. 144: Young
boy; p. 147: Camels grazing; p. 150: Tethered camels; p. 152: Tribal man;
p. 173: Tribal elder; p. 181: Friendly tribespeople.

HarperCollins*Publishers*
25 Ryde Road, Pymble, Sydney NSW 2073, Australia
31 View Road, Glenfield, Auckland 10, New Zealand
77–85 Fulham Palace Road, London W6 8JB, United Kingdom
Hazelton Lanes, 55 Avenue Road, Suite 2900, Toronto, Ontario M5R 3L2
and 1995 Markham Road, Scarborough, Ontario M1B 5M8, Canada
10 East 53rd Street, New York NY 10032, USA

National Library of Australia Cataloguing-in-Publication data:

Williams, R.M. (Reginald Murray), 1908- .
    A Song in the Desert.
    ISBN 0 207 19832 2.
    1. Williams, R. M. (Reginald Murray), 1908- . 2. Australia,
    Central - Description and travel. I. Wade, William. II.
    Title.
919.42044

Printed in Australia by Griffin Press Pty Ltd on 115gsm Matt Art

9 8 7 6 5 4 3 2 1
01 00 99 98

Contents

WILLIAM WADE AND R. M. WILLIAMS
ABOUT TO EMBARK ON THEIR EXPEDITION

Preface

This is a story of William Wade. Born in London, a Cockney, Wade spent his early life as a sailor, was converted by the Salvation Army, migrated to Australia in 1924 and spent the rest of his days as a missionary to the Aborigines.

For three years, from the age of eighteen, I wandered with Wade in the deserts of central Australia. We slept by countless camp fires, seldom the same one. We measured time by the seasons and days by the sun. I had no other company but Wade or sometimes naked Aboriginal hunters of my own age. The smell of desert wood camp fires and the sounds that the desert makes were comforting pleasures that no others have ever matched.

It was a time to set patterns for life.

Some would say the desert is silent. It has its moments: the whispering breeze of the hour before sunrise, the birds making a special music. Lightning explodes and storms roar. The night is never without its tiny insect chirping, and as if from nowhere comes the music of the frogs of the claypans when they know, somehow, of a coming rain. Then when man intrudes the desert is silent for a moment.

Grateful thanks to Thyrza Davey for her stunning artwork and contribution to this book.

R.M. WILLIAMS
1998

Chapter 1

Our Journey Begins

*It was ... almost
unknown country.
Wade had offered to
go into this area,
and I offered to act
as camel driver
and companion.*

Mount Margaret Mission 1925

en came out of the desert naked, natural. No one had yet told them that they needed clothes, or anything else. For many thousands of years the people of the Great Victoria and Gibson deserts had survived. They made their rules using an oral culture — it was not written for these people had not learned to make paper, although some of them had carved wood and made symbols.

Daarbin was the son of Jumbo, or so he claimed — no one from that desert tribe really knew who, of the many who shared the women of the tribe, was his or her sire. Still, every child was allocated to a parental couple. Life went on without dispute about such matters, for rules about mating were strict enough. Death was the punishment for those who coveted a woman of the wrong totem — a breeding system that kept the wandering huntsmen tribes from inbred extinction.

The child Daarbin was thin, almost emaciated. The hunting in the drought had brought the desert people from as far away as a thousand miles to Mount Margaret Mission, near Laverton in Western Australia, a place where rumour told of a white man who gave flour, rice, sugar to any who asked — the corn of Egypt.

Daarbin's tribe had walked for months, crossing others' territories without conflict, for the others — like themselves — had fled the waterless wastes.

To cross the barren spinifex and sand, where small waters had dried up, the women of the tribe had carried on their heads wooden dishes filled with water and dried grass. The grass made body functions possible.

Daarbin, the desert-born, had all the wonders of the whites' world to see, investigate, handle, admire. The music of the Mount Margaret Mission people differed from the corroboree chant, and he liked that. Clothes, cloth, boots — all were new and interesting. Saws, knives, shovels, axes were riches to be coveted. An abandoned tin pot was to be treasured. Everything was wonderful.

Daarbin attached himself to me, Reg Williams, on working days when I was woodcutting and burning limestone to make concrete. He was willing, cheerful, bright as a button. We became friends. I was seventeen, he about ten, but there were things he could do, like making fire with sticks, which were all new to me. Daarbin introduced me to a world which only the desert people knew, of small insects and the life around our workplace.

Sitting at lunch, which I shared with Daarbin, he would show me the tracks left in the dust by many small creatures of the night. Insects, lizards, birds — every track was like a page of information to him. There were those which hurried, those which were being chased, and some species I had never heard of, like the night-active bilby. There were also parrots that flew only at night. Frogs, snakes, centipedes . . . many tracks were there, like a book to read.

I, who in my arrogance believed myself to be educated, found in that quiet desert place that there was a world of knowledge which a ten-year-old could teach me.

Initially, Daarbin did not know my language, but he was quicker to learn mine than I was to learn his. We soon found ways of understanding each other. He would chatter away about the sun going down and the moon rising by pointing to the sun and drawing the crescent moon in the dust. He would point to his foot and name the word for foot. It was a never-ending game; no school was ever so intense. Soon I could say his words for walk, stop, drink, piecing together names for hundreds of surrounding places and articles and actions. Within a month we could converse.

Daarbin became my mentor, introducing me into his tribe — an action which proved to be of great value when I later ventured into his deserts and there found that I was already named and known, for the desert peoples are quick to tell about the ways of strange whites. It is not only their way of gossip, it is their encyclopedia of knowledge.

By 1926 my task at Mount Margaret was completed. The wide, tall water tank that I had been building, made with a concrete mixture of sand, lime and stones, and which I have recently learned is still used today, had been cast into its round shape. It was time for me to go.

I had received a job offer. Quite romantic! And I had an eager need for change. The job had been offered to me by a very religious man. He was a type who did not appeal to my pragmatic idea of what Christian preachers should be. But his proposition was earthy enough. Would I put together a team of camels and take one of his disciples to the unknown 'heathen' tribes of the desert?

It was not necessary to call this a job — it was an adventure. But I never told him just how eager I was to see the wild sandhills and mountains Daarbin had told me about. And I never ever told him how hard it would be to sell religion to the stone-age people of the desert tribes. No young man had ever had so acceptable an adventure offered as a task. I packed up all my concrete tools and my swag and went looking for the nearest camels, which were at Oodnadatta, nearly two thousand miles away by train. I travelled on slow, narrow-gauge rail, but every mile was interesting. All the fellow travellers had stories to tell, and there I was, a young man listening and learning.

London 1924

William Wade, sailor, left his ship at the London dock, intending never to sign on again. And he never did. For a month London was his until his last pound was gone. His last ship had sailed, his drinking mates knew that he was broke and the line of friendship shortened. There was only the army — the Salvos — to offer shelter and a meal once a day, expecting in return, when they beat the drums, to see him at the singing.

Bill liked it when the lads and the lasses clapped their tambourines, beat the big drum and sang hymns. For a man with no ship and no people, the shelter of their obvious goodwill became home — so he joined. A whole-timer Bill, he got religion enough to go out and tell anyone everywhere. How he managed to get to Australia, join a mission and become a preacher to the Aborigines, he never told me. It is a long hike from London to the western goldfields but that's where Wade was when I first met him — a fully fledged apprentice missionary.

A man of many ports, an habitué of portside houses in many countries, he was ready when the time came to be born again — with a wealth of wisdom gained, as comes with knowledge and experience of life.

Oodnadatta 1926

The Australian mission people had called for volunteers to explore the western deserts — Aboriginal tribes were reported to inhabit the Gibson, the Great Victoria and the Great Sandy deserts and what are now known as the Musgrave, the Petermann, the Mann and the Rawlinson ranges. It was a vast area exceeding a million square miles of almost unknown country. Wade had offered to go into this area, and I offered to act as camel driver and companion.

Wade arrived at Oodnadatta from Western Australia in June 1926, in time to collect the supplies — dried vegetables in tins, rice, salt and flour, packed in robust jute (double-bagged) — necessary for our indefinite stay in the remote western deserts. Like me, he had come to Oodnadatta on the rattling old weekly train they called the Ghan, named that way, I suppose, because mainly Afghans used it.

He made his headquarters with a mission team, Harris and Hyde, two devoted women who cared for unwanted half-caste children. I was already staying in the more congenial atmosphere of camel men and gamblers like Bill Gregory and old George Fox. This selection of companions seems to have been the pattern of my life.

There was no feed within many miles of Oodnadatta — thousands of camels and goats had grazed the country bare. This meant camping with my camels far out where there were some trees and bushes suitable for browsing animals. I had learned to live alone, and this was harsh but useful training. One tends to become antisocial if too long alone.

Later on, when the sparsely settled station country was left behind, the tribal lands of the Aborigines, starting at the Musgrave Ranges, brought me into contact with young men of the native people. They soon became my friends and together with the adventure of new places they made for continual interest.

The mission's decision to accept the challenge of sending one of its members to man a Commonwealth expedition was already settled. We would go not as explorers, nor to map the area, but to make contact with whatever tribes inhabited the country bounded by the known coastline areas.

My offer to accompany such an expedition as camel boy was somewhat optimistic, for the little I knew of camels had been occasional meetings with the salt-carrying teams at Underbool while I was burning lime in Victoria. However, as the son of a teamster, the yolking of animals seemed to offer me no great problem.

Wade was given the responsible job of organising supplies for our year or more's scouting trip into the deserts between South Australia and the goldfields of Western

Australia. My job was to purchase camels, break them in for riding and pack-carrying, teach them to work or feed in hobbles, and to obey commands.

Buying Camels

Gool Mahommet, master camel man and the Afghan owner of many working teams, sat outside his primitive camp. His home was a circle of earth-filled tins stacked high. Gool shaded his eyes looking at an unusual visitor, a white boy. He did not speak! As is custom, he waited for the boy to announce his visit.

Not many places on earth are drier or hotter than Oodnadatta, home to fifty Baluchi Afghan teamsters servicing all places north with pioneering necessities.

'My name Williams,' I said. I had been bush long enough to cut words to essentials.

Gool smiled a brief welcome and patted the upturned kerosene tin beside him, indicating that I was to sit. No more words passed between us for the usual time that silent men of the desert take before speaking. Gool waited for me to announce my call.

'I want to buy camels,' I said. The silence that followed was long while I waited for an answer.

'You want cow, bullock, old one, young one?'

The next speech was up to me so, with due reverence to the slow words of barter between the patriarch of cameldom and the youth, I waited the accepted time, then said, 'One big bullock — a leader, three cows, two riding camels with nose pegs.'

The next pause seemed not about to end while I sat waiting in the sun for Gool to answer.

'Five pounds cow. Ten pounds bullock with saddle — old saddle, Seven pounds, old bullock leader. You want packs?'

I waited, as custom requires, pondering the price. This time it was my turn to seem not to have an answer.

'You know camel? '— Gool had asked me the inevitable question.

This one needed a quick reply, so I shook my head slowly, at the same time answering, 'Little bit.'

Gool smiled his slow half smile. He was pleased that I had not boasted.

'I show,' he said, 'tomorrow,' indicating the sun at late afternoon. No price had yet been accepted.

My adviser, Joe Summerfield, was the son of one of the few white camel teamsters. We talked about the price that night and he told me that if Gool had liked me, the deal would be right. No more trustworthy, noble men exist than the fierce Pathan Muhammedan of the desert. Their prayer mat, used every day of their lives in the worship of Allah, is religion at its best.

I was to learn much of the Afghan during the following years, but for the moment my future, perhaps my life, was in the hands of Gool Mahommet.

He had read my lack of experience with camels and found a sincerity which matched his own. The camels he selected for me were such that a desert traveller could trust. The leader was a giant, an anchor. The cows were meek and the saddle mounts nimble. I took delivery with pride, having made a friendship which lasted until Gool's death:

Thus men live and die!

Often, in the night, I hear again 'Allah is great' — the only expression of simple faith that such men as Gool have. When the nights are long and troubled, I repeat, 'Allah is great', and am comforted.

Head of the Rail

In 1926, the camel men who had thrived in the West Australian goldfields at the turn of the century were no longer wanted. Some had drifted north into the Gascoyne area; many had joined their busy Afghan compatriots on the long dusty track, the road through central Australia.

Looking at the map of Australia, I realised that the logical place to launch a camel caravan exploration trip into the western desert was from Oodnadatta, the then head of the rail line from Adelaide.

Located about four hundred miles north of Adelaide and the same distance south of Alice Springs, Oodnadatta was a busy bustling place. Thousands of camels came and went, carrying their loads of merchandise north and west. There were no roads, just a narrow camel pad. Wheel tracks were soon to come, as was the rail north to Alice Springs, but neither roads nor the rail north were built until 1928.

When the rail train unloaded its weekly supply of goods at Oodnadatta, everything was taken into the custody of the merchant store, which was called Wallis Fogarty. A vast store, it held all that the north might need as well as some that was wanted, but perhaps not needed.

The string of one hundred camels winding up the hill to the loading spot behind the blacksmith's shop was an impressive sight. Each camel saddle was left in its nominated spot ready for the Wallis Fogarty staff to deposit the designated load. The team owner would then sort out each saddle and rope and bag it, according to the strength of the camel that would carry it on its long journey north.

I watched, camped on the verandah of the hut belonging to old Bill Gregory. Bill was a man of many parts. At night,

when he was not away with the mail run west or on a trip for his boss, Fogarty, Bill would light the lamp at the end of his long table and throw out the card packs. In that small frontier town, this was the signal for players to gather for a night of poker or, more often, Coo and Can. Old George Fox, a crippled camel man with a chewed-up shoulder, camped there on the verandah, too. Usually, by night George was far under after a day of steady drinking. He was a good friend to me. Bill kept him. They were old-time camel-driving mates.

The Town of Oodnadatta Was Divided

Afghans — camel men, traders, priests, moneylenders — lived west of the rail. Some of them had native wives; most kept a herd of goats. It was an exclusive community — not to say that some were not friendly. They were, but they were also a people apart.

Whites lived close to the rail line. Beside the Ghans, only two white Australians ran camel teams. One of them was almost retired and lived in Oodnadatta; he was a long-time teamster and pioneer bushman called Bagot. The other white camel man, Summerfield, was active in the carrying of freight. It was his son, Joe — the lad my own age — who had advised me in my dealings with Gool Mahommet and who became my friend, an association we maintained for sixty-five years. Being young together, we teamed up when trouble developed, as it does in frontier towns. Joe carried a long, useful knife — a customary tool which was part of a camel man's dress. The nearest I ever came to being a knife man was when Joe taught me to throw a knife accurately — a very dangerous weapon.

Later I would buy a camel from Bagot. However, my next purchase was a half-broke cow from Namoth Khan. Namoth was a kindly man — I liked him. He had a debt to Kabul, the village moneylender, to whom I paid the five pounds for the cow. Other animals were bought after hard bargaining, for then, by careful observation, I knew that I wanted strong unblemished animals of patient temperament — so necessary in the isolation of faraway deserts. I had my troubles with wandering camels in the years to come but never lost any of the several teams I managed.

Memory does not bring them all to mind, but I well recall an incident with a black cow a year later. She developed a grudge after I beat her out of a slippery-sided soakage when she was mad for water. That happened half a continent west of Oodnadatta at a gully in the Mann Ranges. The soakage well was deep and the camels were perishing for want of water, which is why she plunged down the sloping sand, almost burying me.

My pride, however, was a riding camel. A dark-coloured, lightweight racer, she was agile, swift and could match a horse over distance. Another big bullock camel, which became the anchor of the team, came from a deal Gool Mahommet made with Kabul, the moneylender (in my lifetime, it seems, little has changed when debts are being collected).

Why I used 'anchor' as a description of a team leader was because this was a big bullock, and if trouble developed or wild notions made any other camel unmanageable, the unruly one was tied with a stout rope to the big bullock — the anchor. He held them and always managed to tame the wildest, even if unbroken, as were some that we caught.

Here is an interesting comparison of the merits of camels versus horses as a means of travel in Wade's World, as I call the million miles of central deserts we were to explore, by Peter Egerton Warburton, a nineteenth-century explorer:

Note on the Value of Camels in Australian Exploration by Colonel P. E. Warburton

> *It may perhaps be useful to others, should they have an opportunity of getting camels, to know that, in my opinion, they are of all animals the most suitable to Australian exploration. It is quite certain we never should have*

reached the western coast with any others. No doubt in some countries it may be expedient to have horses as well as camels, but this entirely depends upon the character of the country. No horses could have lived with us.

Camels alone can travel over any but a boggy country. Horses alone are useless where there is no feed and little water.

Central Australia is a land of horizons, gibber plains, sandy wastes, distance. A few men love the silent loneliness, as do I, with the comforting thought that no invading peoples will covet these hot dry plains. Perhaps only the Aborigines who, for centuries, have mastered the barren empty places, could call the centre of Australia 'sacred'.

The Bill Wade expedition was to leave from Oodnadatta to seek out amidst the almost unknown deserts the tribes of Aborigines believed to be living in the million square miles of Australia that had still not been exploited in the 1920s.

The so-called 'heathen' were Wade's problem; the camels were mine. Fitting out a self-contained expedition for an indefinite period was a responsible task for which I had little experience. The next year or so would prove that lack.

Nevertheless, I had been raised in the bush and was perhaps as well qualified to survive as most. In time we would discover that our water canteens were not indestructible and that the flour bags could have been treble-covered against wear; the supplies of sugar and salt were meagre; and firearms loads were scanty. When such things as knives and axes got lost, they were irreplaceable in that lonely desert. All these things we would learn the hard way. But this was yet to come.

Chapter 2

Into
the
Unknown

*Wade and I, we were
now in desert lands
far from the settled areas,
towns, rail, police,
shops. We were alone
in an unknown place.*

The Wade Expedition 1926

*T*he camels had been bought, saddles mended, everything was as complete as I could see. It was time for me to hand over to Wade, the boss man. Once in town, Bill Wade took over and I retired into the lowly position of camel boy.

At the end of June 1926, we headed west without fanfare. We silently padded on — a fortnight's walk to the edge of the settled country, then the unknown for another thousand miles — westward, westward, the sun always on our right hand.

I was sorry to leave old Bill Gregory, he had been like a father to me. Only once again did we meet, but such men leave an indelible mark on impressionable youths. He was another of those in whose shadow I have lived my life.

Central Australia was so sparsely settled in the years before a rail line was built from Oodnadatta to Alice Springs that names of almost every person living south of Darwin and north of the Alice were known to all for a thousand miles. All whites lived close to the telegraph line. Roads were camel tracks, and the few wheeled vehicles were mostly pulled by camels — some were horse-drawn, but very few.

West of Oodnadatta for one hundred and sixty miles were the occupied cattle runs. These were primitive affairs, mostly consisting of bough sheds and rough timber yards hitched together with greenhide, which were owner-managed by those hardy pioneers who ran the vast areas without help other than from the Aboriginal tribal people.

Further out, for a thousand miles, lay almost unknown mountains and deserts briefly traversed by explorers who had passed quickly through.

The way west led first to the Alberga River, and we then followed that river to the Musgrave Ranges. Settlers were few — we came across them at 'Todmorton', 'Lanbina', 'Granite Downs' and 'Moorilyanna'. Owners or managers numbered less than a dozen.

As I walked behind the team, there was a certain grandeur about Bill Wade, perched high on a leading camel as the team swung along, like the crusaders with plumes marching to liberate the holy places.

White men of the lonely west met Bill Wade with a sort of cynical restraint. They had attitudes to life that were different from his, especially concerning women. And they resented religious people.

Wade noted their gun belts, with their pistols holstered for ready use. He also noted the aloofness of the spear-carrying Aboriginal men who loitered about the homesteads, almost certainly awaiting some opportunity.

Wade's expedition was well known and talked about — but not favourably. Most of these men had Aboriginal women and were not eager to be told by Wade or anyone else that such an arrangement was wrong. They treated him as a fool, for not many men cared to risk the wrath of the tribesmen in the rugged ranges, and they knew that Bill Wade did not carry a gun.

I, as Wade's boy, was treated the same way they treated Wade — cold and on the outer. It was something I had to live down when I left Wade, but youth enjoys a challenge. Attitudes could and did change.

The first invitation to share a talk and a table came from an old sturdy pioneer one hundred and fifty miles west of the telegraph line. Yes, Mick O'Donough had a harem and he cared not a bit about Wade's sermon on sin. Mick was a hardened soul, ready to make the payment. I liked Mick, and we became friends.

Now Mick's 'Granite Downs' has been given back, with all lands west, to the tribesfolk, which was part of Wade's work. Those lands are now Aboriginal grants.

Wade's Legacy

After three years of exploring, looking, learning, Wade proved his sincerity by dedicating the rest of his life to the desert people. Eventually he set up a depot at Warburton in the Gibson Desert area. And his story, his life, bears the telling, for the end result of it all was a reserve which he explored and which was given to the people he set out to know — a million square miles now belongs to the tribes who have never left it.

The events I relate in the following pages are an introduction to Wade's journey and the years that followed, of his life and work. I believe that in the next centuries Wade's legacy will have a continuing influence on Australia, as it affects the Aborigines of the western deserts. Seventy years have elapsed and already the seeds sown by Wade show signs of a long-term crop. His exploration and fight for Aboriginal land have resulted in a very large reserve which is expanding into an area that will be one-third of the land mass of Australia. That result should see Bill Wade being recognised as the Founding Father of an Aboriginal empire.

Mark this triangle on a map: 'Ernabella', 'Docker River' Aboriginal settlement, Warburton. Take a pair of compasses and swing to include 'Granite Downs', the Everards, the Nullarbor, Laverton and Halls Creek and note that the tribes which were entirely stone-age in Bill Wade's time are now populating this vast area and multiplying. Theirs is not the voice being heard in political circles, but that time will come. Note also that these vast areas could contain the wealth of a nation yet to be born.

I trust that my introduction of Bill Wade as a well-motivated, heroic character will not be interpreted as an attempt to justify the introduction of missions to the desert people, given the disastrous effects that many of those missions have had. I notice today that the strong and virile tribes of the

Birdsville Track have vanished, and that the friendly and sometimes unfriendly tribes of the Cooper and Diamantina have also disappeared. I have well-considered views about the causes and manner of their going.

When I took the job of escorting Wade into the wilds of the Great Victoria and Gibson deserts, I was too young to have such opinions. These conclusions have been formed with a long life of association with the people of the tribes who still survive, and some experience of the causes and effects of the destruction of others.

In the years previous to this story, explorers had made hurried excursions across that long barren land between South Australia and Western Australia. Almost without exception, the diaries of these men told of violent clashes between themselves and the Aborigines.

Neither Wade nor I was literate enough to have read (or heard) of previous penetration into the lands we were to go into, which was as well, because we went without arms of defence or offence. We slept better for it.

'*Moorilyanna*'

At the last outpost of settled country, west of Oodnadatta, end of all roads, was 'Moorilyanna'. Huge granite boulders looked down on a sheltered place. There, too, was a sweet water soakage. It was a small paradise. We filled our canteens with the most exceptional creamy water, the last such that we were to find for many months in a land where waters were brackish, salt, putrid and seldom clean. Clean, pure water is a rare commodity, not only in the desert but now worldwide.

Stan Ferguson, the owner of 'Moorilyanna', the place of sweet water, kept a tidy log cottage — a single room that was elaborate compared with the bough sheds of his neighbours. His wife, a clean, neat half-caste woman, made us welcome.

Sitting at Ferguson's table, we listened to his tales of Aboriginal raids on his stock, attempts on his life. Ferguson believed that he would not have been molested by the Aboriginal people if he had bought or borrowed a full-blood tribal woman. His woman, being a half-caste, was not accepted by the then neighbouring Aboriginal tribespeople.

Stan Ferguson was the last European person we were to see for many months.

Travellers crossing the wide sandy bed of the lonely Alberga River enter another world, leaving all settlements behind. The world seems to expand to an unlimited unknown, at least it did in 1926.

The horizons of the desert, the faraway blue mountains, no roads, no tracks ... not even a footprint of humans or cattle, only the occasional dingo. The tribal lands were still far west. Footprints and camp fires began in the Musgraves:

The empty land brings all men to an evenness where only ability lends status. Some shrink in size, all past elevations vanish; real worth presides.

Black–White Conflict

I was puzzled by the evident absence of the local Aboriginal owners of the land between the occupied station country and the Musgraves, dimly showing in the west, — especially as the country was lush from recent rain.

This was explained later by settlers who would talk — most would not. Tribal people feared the raids of white doggers and others hunting women. The females of the Musgraves were fine-looking girls and obviously lived in fear of the 'blackbirders'.

The first positive evidence of this silent battle between black and white, which was not one-sided, were discarded possessions of white men at the rock hole water. The packs were hanging on a rail — the camp fire was cold and the ashes looked old. There were no bodies.

No doubt some adventurer had made the mistake of thinking that Aboriginal men were helpless. No primitive savage could have been more capable as a silent, skilful hunter than the spearmen of the Musgraves. A man with a gun might be a dangerous enemy but a man with a spear is a stealthy hunter. When possible, the Aborigine took retribution in blood for the invasion of his lands.

I had not realised the depth of feeling that existed in 1926, nor could I have believed that the same subdued hate would become evident now, or might continue as it has done in this past year. Seven decades later, there is still a hatred which will continue to grow unless black and white assimilate into an Australian nation.

New to this unsettled land, we walked on westward towards the Musgraves. Wade eagerly advanced into the unknown. He had no fear that he might be treated as just another white man hunting females and killed accordingly, or perhaps be speared by a man who, as a boy, had seen his father shot by an explorer and was now eager to pay back.

There had been good rain in 1926, bringing lush herbage and a crop of flowering geranium such as has only been seen once in the seventy years since we walked through that garden of sweet-smelling beauty.

This geranium is a desert variety that has a spiral seed like a corkscrew which lies dormant for years or, when a rain comes, stands erect with a mysterious ability, placing its spear-shaped seed into the ground then the cork stem unwinds to bury its seed deep into the wet soil — one of nature's most intriguing and infinitely clever provisions.

The Glen Ferdinand plain was lush with flowering geranium. I have never since seen this plant so deep and luxurious. Only in exceptional seasons does it proliferate, therefore 1926–27 must have been exceptional.

There are seeds like the thistle which blow in the wind, pods like the wattle which explode scattering seed, or burrs that cling to passing animals which carry their seed far away. The subject of seeds is infinite and I would like to expand more on the wonderfully clever patience of nature, but that is another book still to be written.

Pristine in its unstocked natural state, the grasses and saltbush ground covers were still an unexploited treasure.

I am ashamed now to have been the one to tell of these then unknown grazing lands and to be the one to have encouraged Stan Ferguson and Paddy DeConlay to take them up as cattle stations.

But the wrong has since been righted. When the opportunity arose years later, I arranged the purchase of 'Ernabella' in the Musgraves from Ferguson and gave it back to the tribes.

The new problem of the future is the growing population in areas where the Australian Government gives free food to Aborigines without due thought to future locally grown food — creating a nation within a nation without resources.

The Search for Water

Wade and I had between us an old map of Australia which showed the State divisions and prominent features such as the Musgrave Ranges, the Mann Ranges and the towns along the overland telegraph line, like Marree, Oodnadatta and Alice Springs. On the West Australian side, the town of Laverton was marked as a deserted mining area. The gap between Oodnadatta in South Australia, the point of departure for the Wade expedition, and Laverton in Western Australia, was roughly one thousand miles in a straight line. We had a pocket compass, and our intent, after leaving Oodnadatta, had been to go west as far as either the State boundary or the last of the mountains, where we hoped for a permanent water as a depot.

Such waters we found. They were few and far between but, with care, we located these kinds of depot places. From them we could work all points of the compass and, with some fortune, find other waters which would serve as springboards for further travel to meet the tribal people.

This system was elementary yet reasonably safe. So successful was this slow penetration that in time we covered a vast area without either losing our lives or being lost — as others before us had been.

From Halls Creek south to the Nullarbor Plain was roughly a thousand miles. The Great Sandy Desert, as marked on the map, bordered the Gibson Desert on the south, the Gibson Desert in its turn bordered the Great Victoria Desert. Central to those two deserts were the Warburton Range, the Petermann Ranges, the Mann Ranges, the Musgrave Ranges and the Deering Hills.

Wade had been commissioned to study, in detail, the people — How many? Their tribal condition? Attitudes to white intruders? He was to look for waters (if any) and note the type of country, suitability for stock, rainfall. It was quite a commission, covering in excess of a million square miles.

Wade, the sailor turned Salvation Army Christian, was probably the ideal man to meet the unfriendly tribes. He had no ideas about being of a superior race, and he certainly had a kindly attitude.

Months after leaving Oodnadatta, we looked west from the spring at Operinina to the empty lands where an old tribesman had told us of mountains — secrets of the tribe forbade him telling of waters. There had been rain three months before, and so there was a chance that rock holes would still have water in them. If not, the return would depend on how many days we travelled without finding camel water. Our drinking water we carried in steel cans.

We would leave a good water, explore for a few days and, if we found no water, we would return to the security of the place we knew. Sometimes we would go waterless for longer than was prudent, which meant a struggle to get back.

Although the junior, it was accepted that I rode or walked in the lead of the single file of laden camels, reading the earth as some men read books, alert to the track of a wild dog, an emu, sometimes hoping that a footprint would not belong to a man who might lie in wait with intent to kill. I was always watching for little birds whose presence indicated water, or the track of women with children whose direction would indicate a walk towards water.

Emus range far and wide. Often fifty miles from water, they are the furthest-ranging creatures of the desert. A well-worn dingo pad, if fresh, was a promising sign, except that one could not tell whether it was to or from water. We learned to find water in the roots of the acacia tree, but that supply was not enough for camels. Nevertheless, it was good to know it was there if the need arose.

As Wade and I made our perilous adventures into unknown waterless places, I was forever looking for possible waters to retreat to in case of failure to find a destination with water, or in case it was too late for the camels to be saved. This never happened, but I was ready for it.

Scattered in the desert, in the most unlikely places, there are rocks that have become pitted from centuries of erosion and which hold water from rains. It is often tainted, sometimes putrid, but I had my ways of cleaning such water enough to save our lives. Boiling and condensing the steam at night, filtering it through charcoal, pouring it through sand — it never lost its taint, but it was water.

Native wells are mostly hidden to protect their tribal owners, but always there are signs left by the users.

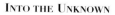

I became adept at locating the soakage wells. Sometimes these were shallow, but often they were too deep to dip in. One had to climb down and this was risky.

Trees, which are hollow, are scarce in the desert, but the desert oak is one tree that flourishes in odd places and some of them have hollows that collect water. Dry creek beds have cool bars which, on rare occasions, have water in hollows.

I found out that the claypan frogs go underground as the waters dry up. They are large and take down a body of water in their stomachs which yields enough to save a perishing traveller. Finding their retreat is a skilled business which luckily the native boys taught me.

In the desert there would be places where tribes had dug for yams. Night animals over a fresh track meant that the track had been made the day before. A clean, fresh-cut track or a burning ember of bark meant the maker was close by, probably hiding. Tracks were a book we had to learn to read.

I could sense that the new Bill Wade of the desert and the camp fire, so recently migrated from the sea, was beginning to see that his new Master was also one *with* those that he, Wade, considered sinners. But never one *of* them. Perhaps his realisation that 'separation was not sainthood' had brought him to seek out the lowliest primitive people, and to make an effort to share their life, which he did with 'his Aboriginals'. I believe that this lately converted sailor never quite accepted the fact that Jesus was a friend of sinners. In his eyes, every white man he met was a sinner.

It is a long step for any man to come off the pinnacle of feeling he is a unique and chosen one of God's children to

realising that all men and women are equal in God's eyes. I do believe that when Wade first headed west he thought that the Aborigines were low in the eyes of God. But he learned in time that God valued the people whom Wade had looked on as 'heathens'.

Confessions by the Camp Fire

Wade and I, we were now in desert lands far from the settled areas, towns, rail, police, shops. We were alone in an unknown place. All about us were old camp fire sites, footprints of men, women and children, but no sighting of the naked tribespeople who had made them.

No doubt we had been followed, observed, talked about in their councils and they'd concluded that we were harmless. We showed no signs of weapons, did not keep watch at night and never chased females as other whites had done. We were alone in their country and they could wait.

Wade and I sat by the camp fire and talked, which was unusual because he and I had little in common. I was a lad without experience. He had trodden the streets of London and Shanghai, shared the wild and wilful ways of reckless men and knew the devious ways of men's and women's depravity. He was a man of the world. I was nothing, a camel boy. But sometimes he talked, not boastfully, almost ashamed to admit his past depravity. I was an eager listener.

Perhaps Bill's conscience never let him rest, for although he was a made-over man with his new religion, no man fully believes that the past is forgiven. I had no past to forgive, but was eager to earn something to look back on.

I was a child of the open places, a son of pioneers. Bill was a product of the slums of Bow Bells in London. We had a lot of catching up to do in understanding one another. But there was no one else.

Neither he nor I could speak the Aboriginal tongue. They were stone-age, naked hunters, homeless wanderers. Here again, there was a lot to learn for them and for us.

Bill and I spent many long months alone by the camp fire with our six camels, provision for a year or more, a vast desert to explore and, for Bill, the vision splendid; himself a 'saved' man sheltering under the immortal flag.

A happy man, Bill — he was obsessed by his ambition to take 'saving' to the Aboriginal wanderers in the wild.

His stories were about his days at sea, the cruel imprint of debauchery stamped on the faces and actions of the drifters, the people — 'sinners' Bill now called them. All that was behind him now; Bill was a saved man and it seemed so. No temptation could move him, nothing at all could deviate this product of the wandering life from his mission. His story became monotonous for me then, but the idea lives on, for I am convinced that his dedicated spirit has stayed with me.

Seventy years have passed since we shared the camp fire among wandering people and wild lands. I am inclined to believe now that those who give body and soul to Christ are made over — 'saved' — treat the word as you will. It was clearly defined in William Wade, the former sailor.

Wade would never have been rated as either a bushman or a horse-breaker. He was always in trouble, either getting lost himself or losing his camel. But compare, if you will, the end result. Harry Bell Lasseter, who was in the ranges at the same time as us, not only lost his camels, but also his life. Alf Gibson, that honoured bushman after whom the Gibson Desert was named, lost his animals and his life. Paul Edmund de Strzelecki wandered the same deserts and was heard from no more.

Without help from me or anyone else after I left him, Wade went out from Laverton in 1929 and found, and eventually pioneered, Warburton mission.

Those who have never slept in the windswept spinifex sandhills, sheltered in a cave or drunk from the muddy waters of Aboriginal soaks can never know the Wade who lived by the new light which burned in him. This tough little

Cockney never cared where he slept or what tomorrow might bring. He was changed all right.

Sitting by the camp fire, Wade's mind often took him back to the waterfronts thronged with seamen hunting ships, every man hungering. Strange that narrow gap which gives protection by codes of law, arranged to protect the haves from the have-nots, that fine line of moral behaviour that seems to get less important when hunger drives a man, as it had Wade. Bill did not speak often about those nights when the only way to eat was to turn thug, risking everything for a bite of food. There were no regrets for the change he'd made, and no regrets for anything of the sea — the new ports, new women.

There were nights when Bill did speak, but often he would slip into silence or walk away from the fire to pray alone. If he did not come back I would light a beacon fire to guide him to the camp. There are no signposts in the desert; out there lie the bones of many brave men who perished alone in the wide, open country.

Some would say that Wade was an incurable romantic. Don't write him off like that — this man who would lay his life on the line in a faith so illuminated.

There were no roads, no tracks where Wade and I went, and no known waters. Tribes were sometimes hostile, with medicine men who brooked no foreign God. Men who, for long centuries, had practised death by the pointing of a bone. Into this unknown land Wade went, believing. He had that sort of faith.

Often the day would end with our meal at the camp fire — just a rabbit stewed in the pot or baked on the fire. The time came when Wade had used or given the food we had, bringing us to share an emu leg or a kangaroo tail soup.

His pity for the aged ones left to die, or those with wounds or burns needing more care than pity could provide, made me party to a charity I had not learned.

Somewhere in the sound of Bow Bells near the London wharfside, where Wade had changed direction, he had learned the Salvo's songs, the hymns of the saved. His accent was Cockney, and his voice was partly out of tune, but on every opportunity he sang those very symbols in his new life. There must be men who were boys then, who now, between corroborees, sing 'Rock of ages cleft for me' or 'Wide wide is the ocean, deep as the deep blue sea', Wade's favourite hymn.

After all, perhaps religion is all spirit and who knows . . . Perhaps the preacher of no cathedral or chalice saw Wade of the blue yonder as his favourite priest. I can see Wade now bending over the rotting flesh of an old woman in the last stages of the leprous yaws, praying for her.

The singing crusade, which Wade kept up all his life, had a fine effect on the Aboriginal children, for it was in the words and spirit of those songs that those who did not understand his message found something unique and, having learned his songs, never forgot them. Seventy years later, I sometimes find myself singing the words and making an attempt at the tunes.

The Aboriginal people in the white-settled areas of Australia, who are descendants of the once tribal Aborigines and have long since been used to European food, have lost the abilities of the wild.

The 'do-gooders'? No! That's a harsh judgement. The 'kind hearts' — that's better — are busy trying to help the descendants of the Aboriginal tribes.

It is becoming alarmingly evident that the politicians and media are not aware of the vast area now allocated to the Aboriginal people of central Australia. Some of it, in fact most of it, is rated as semi-desert — the Great Victoria Desert, the Gibson Desert, the Great Sandy, together with the Musgrave Ranges, the Mann Ranges, the Petermann, Warburton, Everard, and many minor ranges. Note that the area bounded by 'Granite Downs' on through the Everard Ranges stretches for a thousand miles to the goldmining areas of Western Australia. The country included in that mallee desert north of the Nullarbor Plain to the fringe of the Kimberley is free to the indigenous tribes. Not all is gazetted as Aboriginal reserves but most of this vast area — approximately a third of the land mass of Australia — is used by them, if they wish, as hunting ground.

Wade had a favourite quotation. Where Wade got this quotation is a mystery to me, for it was used by an English king years later. And it is this:

And I said to the man at the gate of the year
'Give me a light that I may go safely into the unknown.'
And he replied
'Put your hand into the hand of God. It shall be to you better
than a light and safer than a known way.'

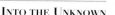

Chapter 3

Desert Survival

*Wade and I headed
south in 1927 from a
water on the eastern end
of the Mann Ranges.
The water was a deep
soakage well which
we had excavated*

The Dream World

The desert tribes are an old, old race of people; spiritual, one might say. On first contact, the impression I got was of an earthy race of basic survivors. But there is more. They had a developed relationship with the earth, the animals, and all about them, in an understanding and spiritual feeling which far exceeded any culture I have yet found among the proud materialistic peoples of other nations.

Every place, every plant, every happening was part of a God-created environment so wrapped up in their own lives as to make them part of a world in which they were one with a mysterious and total earth.

Nothing in the religions of the world wraps mankind in a completeness with the earth as does the dream world that the Aborigines claim has descended from what they look back to and call the Dreamtime.

I am not deluded by a need to enter such a cocoon of comfortable mystery, and I am persuaded that there is a larger understanding of the eternal. Nevertheless, it pleased me as a youth, with these brilliant survivors but child-like people, to share their beliefs in the wonders of the storm, the wind, and all that we can see and feel. These things are evidence of creation, as are we.

Perhaps — even surely — there are windows into an unexplored world of the spirit. We know that there is a great mystery behind the dark curtain of our dim understanding, something we cannot measure, weigh or calculate, but we cannot deny. Or, if we do, the price is a darkness where hopelessness is akin to death.

The wanderer in the desert pondering the great mystery of life, so seemingly pointless, may never have had the chance to read the manuals of spiritual guidance in any holy book but, they can hear the words of songs that speak. All Bill Wade could ever explain, probably all he knew himself I believe, was the very simple saying that 'God was in Christ'. Summed up, he could never explain the cross as a symbol to an illiterate people who had never met a carpenter or seen a nail or known a Caesar.

The heathen — if most of the world may be called heathen, oppressed, burdened, lost in the mysteries of life — can find freedom, comfort and a guiding light in a 'Creator who cares', once they are free of their traditions. I can understand Wade, as he tried the almost impossible. But I know that the spirit of this man was like the spirit of light in a dark place which, after all, was enough. As time and more than half a century has proved, they — his flock — roam millions of wild acres of their own land without the fearful taboos of past ages.

For the tradition of the past weighs like an alp on the brain of the living. (Marx)

Bill Wade helped shift that weight.

Tall Men

This vast area, where Wade and I travelled, was a little-known part of Australia in 1926. The expeditions I have named, plus a few isolated attempts to examine parts bordering it, were exploration journeys rather than organised contact with its tribal people. When the east–west rail line was built from Port Pirie to Perth, the natives coming down to the line from the Musgraves were still entirely naked and as primitive as the coastal tribes a century before. This was due to the isolated, unwatered, desert type of country which presented a hazardous problem of supply and other serious obstacles such as the dense mallee tree scrubs above the Nullarbor. The vast, straight bare plain was in itself a problem because, at that time, it was reckoned to be waterless. The Willorara tribe north of the plain knew of one deep cave on the Nullarbor and had exploited it for centuries as a place of refuge.

These deep mysterious limestone caves go down to unexplored depths. Some have been briefly examined, but the dangers of the dark pits, wandering caverns and deep waters offer a challenge to the future.

Some of these, or at least one such cave, has been a refuge for the Willorara tribe for a timeless past — a haven.

I learned this previously well-kept secret of the cave when Akbar Khan, the Afghan man who later became my friend, paid for a half-caste woman (or girl, I should say, as she was very young). When he purchased Lali, she told him of the usage made of the Nullarbor cave in time of flight from invading war parties who regularly raided her mother's tribe, the Willorara. When her people became aware that strange hunters had entered their territory, signals were sent to all females, old men and children to flee south to the prepared refuge in this cave. Deep in its subterranean depths, there was water and food in the form of dried seed, wild figs and dried quandongs, that had been stored. The cave was a mysterious hollow cavern where strange noises could be produced, giving eerie sounds which invaders, in their superstitious primitive fearfulness, avoided. The women, old men and children stayed there until the fighting males of the tribe gave the 'all clear'.

It is known that the Aboriginal tribes dried the flesh of quandongs and small desert figs, pressing the dried fruit into blocks which were wrapped in bark and stored in caves. Seeds of the grasses available, of which there were several, were also stored in wooden coolamons. I have eaten their grass-seed cakes. They are gritty — almost tasteless — real survivor food.

In their flight from invading tribes, the smaller, thus weaker, desert Aborigines had devised ways of escape that were effective. They were probably developed over centuries of attack by the stronger fierce warriors of the northern ranges. Being a scattered people, hunting over an area about the size of England, there was not a lot of opportunity for Wade and I to meet them, but some did overcome their timorous fear of strangers. One family of three men with their women, children and old ones contacted us after days, probably weeks, of observing us from secret hiding places. The men were the tallest of all Aborigines we had met, or any I have seen since. Two of them would exceed six feet, six inches (1.95 metres) and the other man was over six feet (1.83 metres). They were slim but well formed. Such an isolated tribe — they were bounded on the south by the Nullarbor and hemmed in on the west by the Great Victoria Desert.

The Tribes

There was very little surplus fat on the migrating hunters of the Aborigines of the deserts. In a good season, the upper arms of the men were heavily muscled because their

livelihood depended on throwing skills, but the legs of all desert people were very thin. In a good season, the only visible surplus was carried on the back. Constant walking would, of necessity, keep the legs and buttocks slender. The very young sometimes were the most chubby as these were carried by mothers on the long hot migrating journeys. I have seen a woman carry two very young ones for long hours over rough country.

There was enmity between the weaker tribes of the south and the stronger tribes of the northern ranges. This, coupled with their perfect breeding program of selective totems has produced a race of survivors who have no equal on earth. The desert nature of their lands, coupled with their total lack of animal or mechanical transport, has bred a race of people who can live where only other desert-hardened mammals could survive.

When Akbar Khan was telling me of the tribal flights from the spinifex and mallee country to the shelter of the Nullarbor caves, we decided that some day he and I would ask his girl to guide us to see these mysterious caves. Even then I knew that the powerful taboo of tribal fear — deep in the very life of the females — about revealing tribal secrets, would probably stop her telling even us about them. This expedition was never made.

The vast south lands between the Musgrave and the Mann ranges and the great plain called the Nullarbor is so dense, so big, that Wade determined to examine those thick mallee-covered scrubs to see how many tribal people inhabited that part which has been named — wrongly, some argue — the Great Victoria Desert. Wade and I headed south in 1927 from a water on the eastern end of the Mann Ranges. The water was a deep soakage well which we had excavated to a depth of about twelve feet. The soakage well seemed permanent enough to use as a base camp if we could not find water in the southern Victoria Desert. Others had declared this area waterless, but our experience by now indicated that where people lived there had to be water, and from time to time we could see smoke far south.

Our first attempt to penetrate the Great Victoria Desert was successful when we found water on the fifth day of our east and south travel (perhaps a hundred to one hundred and twenty miles). The water was contained in deep pits on a flat sandstone slab about an acre in extent. There were people there, but they were very shy and try as we would, we could not coax them into our camp.

There were interesting desert animals and birds living in those southland scrubs. Wallabies of a rare type lived on isolated rocky outcrops. The spinifex contained numberless small mouse-like creatures which were pouched, and were night animals. The white bilby, also a night animal, was there. We found the people who later joined us hunted this bilby for its white tasselled tail to use as an ornament and, of course, to eat. Some emus ranged the desert but few kangaroos lived in the scrubs. Foxes were there as well as some rabbits, and also an occasional squatting miniature-type kangaroo, also pouched. These we found easy to catch for, like rabbits, they would stay crouched in their squat. Quail-like birds lived in the desert, usually about a dry claypan. We made a point of noting the birds, which water regularly, because at evening they would be flying towards water. There were numerous types of pigeons, including the spinifex pigeon — small

brown squat birds with a stumpy tail and stripes down the back. Near waters there were finches, of a type which I was not experienced enough to name. Hawks and eagles ranged the vast scrublands.

Gold

I later heard that somewhere west of these timbered wastelands were quartz outcrops which showed gold, but in all the many journeys Wade and I made into the Great Victoria Desert, we never sighted any gold-bearing quartz. It's a big, big country and we could not see it all in detail. Nevertheless, we tried.

As to the gold reefs described by Lasseter, who died in the Petermann Ranges, it is doubtful if he ever collected any samples, for there were never ever any shown by him after earlier trips.

Wade and I were travelling to the far south and east of the Petermann Ranges at the time that Lasseter died, but the native peoples we were in contact with never told us of him. Perhaps our southern tribes were not friendly with the Petermann folk.

Somewhere in that very large Victoria Desert there is an outcrop of high-grade gold reef from which came the samples which prompted our later attempt to look for gold. Neither Wade nor I during our travels found gold. The high-grade samples belonged to Jim Prince. About him there will be more as this book is written.

My other evidence of a rich gold reef was told to me by Akbar Khan, who had hurried through the same desert area. The Great Victoria Desert is so large and so dry that exploration in detail would be difficult and, being somewhat featureless, it is hard to find particular locations.

Travelling with Wade through the western deserts was not exactly leisurely because of the distance from water to water — or the need to look for such water. Therefore it is unlikely that we would have had time to look for gold. Nor

were we at that time experienced in detecting mineral-bearing rocks for, as I found in later years, there are many types of rocks and soils which carry gold.

Tennant Creek, on the eastern side of the Tanami Desert, is made up of many types of gold-bearing rock and clay. The main reefs, which I later worked with success at Tennant Creek, were haematite, a hard grey rock interspersed with crushed oxidised-looking soft burnt oxides, which was a rich producer.

The chief gold reefs of the area north of Kalgoorlie were quartz. The largest deposits of gold found on all continents has been so varied that one would need to test samples all along the way. Wade and I could never have stopped on our travels between waters to examine for gold.

If there was a great rich reef in our deserts — and I have the word of two good men for it — I certainly did not find it. Jim Prince showed me his gold and told me where he got it, but Jim never did get back to the right spot. Akbar Khan told me of a reef showing free gold. He also never went back. The desert is a fearsomely large place.

I Meet an Old Camel Man

Those were the days before the advent of roads, cars, trucks and planes to the centre of Australia. Men used to refer to themselves proudly as 'a horseman', 'a teamster' or 'a camel man' back in 1926. It is now 1998, seventy-two years later, as I write about that long ago time when we were young and eager to fight the world. I had never hoped to meet again anyone of those early days. Imagine my surprise then, just ten minutes before I sat down to recollect and write about these times, when a call came from a grandson of my old fatherly friend, Bill Gregory — the camel man.

Tomorrow, he said, he would bring his father — as old or older than I — to meet me again. This, for me, is an epic occasion as no doubt meeting people from long ago is to everyone who grows old and remembers.

In 1926, I had taken a job which was a man's job, and I was a boy without skill. The men all about me were desert-wise and old in the toughest animal-handling trade there is. They were camel men — dark, bearded, turbaned men who seldom spoke. And I needed a friend very badly, for the job I had taken was to buy and equip an expedition which could last months or even years.

It was the old camel man, Bill Gregory, father of my visitor, who had rescued me. Now the visit is over, I know his son is the same age as me, almost to the month. He also had been a camel man, and we had a lot to talk about.

Doctor Cedric Gregory, a man who attended a one-teacher school at Oodnadatta, had worked his way up from earning a pound (two dollars) a week as a camel boy to keeping himself in schools until he achieved a doctorate in mining engineering.

He was the eldest son of the old camel man who had befriended me, advised, taught and sheltered me through those months when I had to do what I was simply not experienced to do.

We talked the hours away about the old Afghans who lived in his home town, and the Chinamen who made gardens on the water holes close to Oodnadatta.

It seemed that C. E. Gregory and I were the only ones living who could remember the transition from camels to trucks at Alice Springs, and the Oodnadatta days when it was the end of the line, when the Alice town was not more than a pub and police depot.

What an accomplishment Bill Gregory, the camel man, achieved in his son, C. E. Gregory.

Chapter 4

The Great Beyond

I often missed the camaraderie of the quiet stockmen. I missed the talk or the silent communion around the camp fires.

Wade's Language

*P*assing through stations, Wade never did learn to find common ground to talk, nor did he learn to comprehend the language of silent communion used by the lonely pioneers who seldom met other whites. Most, almost all, the men who patrolled the unfenced cattle runs had Aboriginal companions, Aboriginal girls. The prejudice of mission folk had rubbed off on Bill Wade, who had no hesitation in declaring the ways of unmarried whites sinful. This continued to make travelling with him very hard for me because I often missed the camaraderie of the quiet stockmen. I missed the talk or the silent communion around the camp fires.

The language of people, places and nations does not all run to the spoken word; although the spirit of communion changes from place to place.

Wade did not have this with whites, but he had it in a big way with the blacks. The waving of hands, smiles, songs and simple goodwill were Wade's language which, in the almost opposite way, was the body language of the lonely cattle men, those who never learn in schools and never become accepted by the codes of society.

I am not wrong in my acceptance or agreement with those lonely men who pioneered the lands far beyond civilisation. White women seldom followed the original pioneers of the loneliest outposts. Those who did often found that they had been preceded by girls of the indigenous people.

The station country in that remote area was still in its pioneering state; bough sheds to live in for the most part, with the workforce peopled by tribesmen who either belonged to that place now or had previously.

The explorers' diaries tell of straightforward travels from east to west or, in the case of explorer David Carnegie, from south to north and return. The explorers who had made these passages across land, unexplored by Europeans, had survival in the unknown as their daily objectives. Unlike the explorers, we were not to travel swiftly through the vast deserts from north to south or east to west, but were to go wherever we could take an intimate look at the people living there, gathering some estimates of their numbers. The missions and the other interested bodies, such as the Lands Departments of Western Australia and South Australia and the Northern Territory and Commonwealth statisticians, had decided to make the survey of Aboriginal peoples the prime objective of the Wade expedition.

You might well ask: 'What is this vast kingdom?' I was going to say, 'that was given to the Aborigines', but that would be wrong. It was always theirs and, without being taken or settled by whites, has remained as the hunting ground of the people, or 'tribes', who traditionally owned it.

The South Australian portion, of which the Tomkinson Ranges occupy the extreme north-west corner, was triangulated by Carruthers 1888–92, a period of four years. During that time he had made field sketches which were not available at the time Wade and I looked over this area in detail. Perhaps it was just as well for the rock holes marked in his sketches would have been after rainwaters and, from our experience, dangerous to rely on. At no time did we ever find evidence of his camps except the trig on his highest point, Mount Woodroffe.

A creek runs out of 'Ernabella' and the Glen Ferdinand area, which was joined about twenty miles down on its southern leg by a creek running out of the Mount Woodroffe watershed. Both these creeks empty out into samphire bush flats south-west of the Everards. This is barren country, the sandhills on the west of Officer Creek run north-west–south-east as we found to our considerable grief coming back to the Musgraves from a journey to the far south about the Deering Hills. The sand hills were right across our path. They are spaced about one hundred yards apart and, although not high, the cover of spiky spinifex makes them wearisome, and when the spinifex has not been burned lately the going is very prickly, especially for one walking and leading camels.

Without spinifex, Australia would be another Sahara. The sharp plant has many uses. First, it saves a large part of Australia from erosion by drifting sands, and it is the shelter for small animals and birds. It provides the gum for spear points and stone-sharpening tools on the woomera handle and, in settled areas, the seed stems are useful cattle fodder.

Eddie Conellan, the founder of our famous pioneer air service, Conellan Airways, which served the people of the central and desert areas, once declared spinifex to be Australia's most valuable plant. Its tenacious fibres hold the earth in place and prevent its fragile components from blowing away and flowing into the wasting sea.

In our second year, travelling east, we were close by the place I've just described when we experienced a different kind of storm. All dark clouds are not rain clouds. All deserts are subjected to dark rolling storms which are not rain storms. A huge dark ball on the horizon, which creeps closer with a rolling motion, is how the terrible dust storm comes. They are not common, only two such have been my lot and both were terrible experiences. Others have told me of such storms with the same frightening experience.

On this trip, Wade had taken one of his 'life in hands' trips into the far southern Victoria Desert area. Only a small water, barely enough to keep camels alive, had rescued us on the extreme south end of this exploration. Now it was time to retreat to a known water, far away to the north. We were returning from this trip when the dust storm hit us. We were desperate for water and expected to find it at Erliwanyawanya, the rock hole that Arthur Treloar, the owner of 'Ernabella', had mentioned as being on the south side of the Musgraves.

Following an all-night crossing of the sandy spinifex ridges to the water which was to be our salvation, we ended at an empty rock hole long known to be a permanent water. Dry — all that was left was mud. Faint dog tracks showed that the hole had been dry for a week or more. We were shattered. Wade was like Moses in the wilderness pleading God to help his people. Wade was no Moses but every mortal feels betrayed at some time in life, even those who daily walk hand in hand with God sometimes doubt.

I quote King David and later the Most Famous King of all, Jesus Christ:

Eli, Eli Lama Sabachthani?

(My God, My God, why hast thou abandon me?)

I could almost expect to hear Wade making this age-old cry when he found the big water dried up.

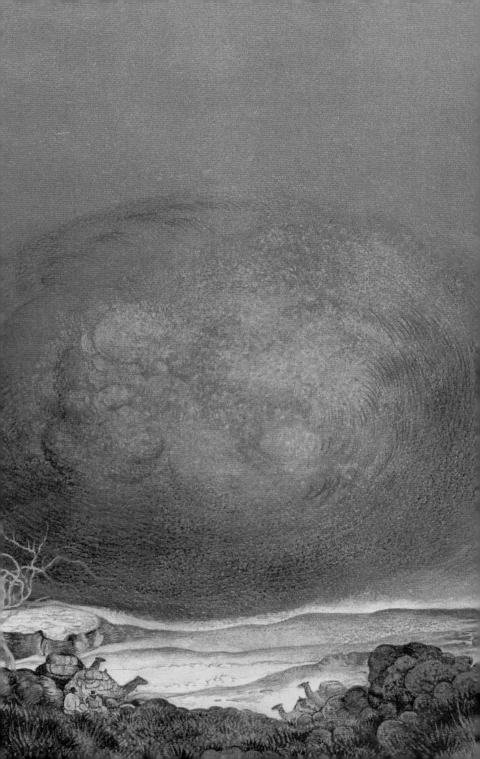

Still early in the day, we had no alternative but to travel to the last known water, thirty miles to the east, a long way for perishing camels. It was hard going, for we who had only visited the next water once and that a year before. The hope was that at the end, we would find animal tracks going to water. By late afternoon, the country looked familiar. One should always look back in trackless country for the outlook is different. It was a lesson I learned the hard way because everything looked strange going east when our last look had been going west. A gap in the ranges was my landmark. If I could find the gap, the water was somewhere near. Then it was that the phenomenon we had barely noticed, a rolling dust storm, came up from the west and rolled over us.

Day turned to night, so black that one could not tell that a camel was following, except by the pull on the nose line. A hand held up to the face was barely visible, sharp sand and gravel cut as it whirled past. Fortunately the wind was from the west on our backs as we were going east, otherwise travel would have been impossible. We plodded on. At the worst of the storm I fell onto my knee tripping over a pad. It was the pad we had made on the first west-going journey.

Camels strung out make a deep pad in single file as they walk one behind the other leaving the crusty desert earth imprinted into a narrow path about a foot wide. This pad we followed through the lessening dust into the gap in the ranges. I shall remember, always, falling into that cool water with clothes still on, the camels pressing behind for a drink.

Wade and the Aboriginal Supernatural

All stone-age people had a strong affinity with the supernatural and none more so than the children of the Australian deserts. It concerned all that which they could see and hear. The roll of thunder as the voice of God: would you disagree with that?

Get out into the black night where the clash of thunder is like giant whips cracking. The night, brilliant with lightning that does not cease, is alive. If you do not shudder, fearful, then it has not been your lot to see the animals, humans and trees slashed to the ground. Remember that the Aborigines have no houses, few caves. They fear the elements as the hand of God. The mighty swirling dust storms, which roll over everything, smothering with their mantle of sand, are fearsome. Crouch in the lee of a rock, hands covering the face, scarce able to breathe. Not even a hand visible. That is how real dust storms are. Imagine the terror of people who know no home. That again is the mysterious power of a force.

The homeless Aboriginal tribesman feels but cannot explain. Even you who know it all, enlightened, will sometimes cry in emergency. To whom? I have seen strong, faithless men, stricken in great storms, cry out a prayer to a God they do not know. I have seen this fear in men who claim no religion. Especially in a great storm at sea, these strong, faithless men cry to a God they do not know. Let us then not despise the untutored primitive peoples who worship at shrines which are invisible powers beyond human conception.

The Unlettered Man

By the camp fire, through months of lonely wandering, never once did I see Wade attempt to read a Bible, if he had one. Probably Wade, the Cockney sailor, had never bothered to master the written word. I say this because it illustrates the simplicity of his faith, not unlike that of a stone-age untutored Aborigine. Here was a man who had so lately accepted the word of a preacher, who told of a man long ago crucified for his love of a lost world. None of the finer points so fiercely fought by Christians of all creeds had contaminated Wade's acceptance of an unseen gift. His was a new life of believing. That simple faith appealed to me — and still does!

That vast so-called 'heathen' world — India, China — stands aghast at the divisions of Christendom. Ghandi, the Hindu, that martyr for India, often laying his life on the line, nearly fasting to death for the freedom of his people, had one supreme hero, one like himself, ready to lay down his life; his favourite hymn, concerned that man so long dead, so much alive forever, Jesus, the one who said:

And I, if I be lifted up, will draw all men unto me.

Ghandi said:

When I survey the wondrous cross on which the Prince of Glory died, my richest gain I count but loss, and pour contempt on all my pride.

When Wade made his historic move into the great deserts, he did not know that his work would create an empire larger in area than many countries of Europe. Nor did he live to see the rise of his people to claim their identity as an indigenous people — not as tribes, but as a nation. We have yet to see the final result of this.

The Light

You will note that this book was illustrated by Thyrza Davey. (Some of you very old readers might remember the wonderful illustrations in *Hoofs and Horns* magazine published almost fifty years ago. Those paintings were done by Thyrza Davey in her teens.)

When this book was mooted as a history of the Christian mission man, Bill Wade, Thyrza offered to use her considerable ability and knowledge of the Aborigines to illustrate the pages.

I have had other books for which she would not paint because she claimed they were not in line with her faith.

Some people wander down many roads to no destination, others learn that ideas and ideals are the roads to travel.

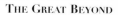

The painting 'The door, the light' is Thyrza's idea, on which she has spent many long hours. She sees Christ as the light of the world and one who knocks at many doors. I agree that this is a great painting and am sure that it illustrates Wade's mission. Thyrza believes that my cynical attitude towards a man preaching to a people who cannot understand, is wrong.

Perhaps one does not have to see or hear to know kindness of spirit. This may well be so.

Wade Takes His 'Light' to the People of the Desert

What will happen to those people still living in the desert? That is the question asked by a doubting world. What can the Christian offer the 'heathen', as they were spoken of, these Aboriginal people?

No doubt Wade would shrug this question off as an irrelevancy. From my own past I have often searched for an answer that would shed more light on the most important question ever posed. Men and women of all ages have held eager hands to heaven asking for a light that will take them into the unknown. The answer given by the self-appointed keepers of 'the way', who speak from the pulpits of many creeds, would find it hard to explain the mysteries of any religion to a stone-age people, living from day to day on the bounty of nature, sometimes brutal and harsh.

This was the task Wade set himself, and this was how he tried to interpret his God of forgiveness and understanding. An old woman, dying and abandoned by her people, sees only the comfort of sympathy and kindness as the Hand of God. The oppressed, by want and hate and fear, know only a friendly hand as the Hand of God. These were the visible interpretations of Wade's new faith in a world of an unknowable eternity. Is there anything more?

If you knew the strange paths of the homing birds which travel the earth in a routine that has no known directive, fish that invade half the oceans to return by dangerous rivers to spawn, or how the mighty power of a measurable but unknown current can light a city, then you might perhaps understand the world we live in. For now, we are still on the fringes of understanding.

Some of the earth's primitives still hold powers that have modern man puzzled. I have seen the mystics of India defy gravity, watched while they grew a tree from seed while I stood there, an unbelievable feat, which no one could make me doubt, with my eyes seeing it and my hand holding the leaves.

Messages have crossed vast distances from stone-age man to tribes far away. The details were not in smoke signals, the information was too complicated for smoke.

All these things, which we find hard to understand, pale into insignificance beside the power of Love and Charity which have the power to change lives, build nations and seemingly represent a spirit which has something to do with creation.

The Missions

Briefly, here is a description of the state of the Aboriginal people in the early 1920s. It makes a shameful, depressing, but well-documented picture, and for the reason of credible record, and I emphasise Wade's work towards the establishing of the desert kingdom, I will record the unfortunate happenings and state of the Australian occupation.

By the turn of the century, Tasmania had ceased to be an Aboriginal island. Victoria too was scarcely populated by any cohesive tribal people. South Australia now had two small tribes living stone-age in the north-west corner, also a disjointed small group of mixed half-caste people in the Point

Pearce, Port Augusta and Flinders area. New South Wales had been entirely occupied by white settlers leaving small enclaves of mixed half-caste and original Australians no longer under tribal law. The Kimberley in Western Australia has been occupied by pastoral holdings employing Aboriginal stockmen with loosely connected tribal affiliations, the whole area policed by whites, tribal laws disregarded. Labour in the area is still supplied by stone-age tribesmen and women from the desert area. The Catholic mission at Balgo in the Halls Creek area had, for half a century, protected Aboriginal interests. The priests were good men, parochial in attitude, so their influence did not extend far south. (The Balgo Mission is now government-controlled.)

The area around Darwin has a large gathering at Port Curtis and more than a few at settlements south-west of the Victoria River. The people of the Kakadu, Northern Territory and Queensland Gulf area are multiplying right across to the Peninsula. Half-castes and a few old-timers have multiplied at such places as Murgon and Palm Island. It could be safely said that all those so named are living on government state and federal bounty and have no alternatives but to stay as dependants of the states or join into the wider multi-race culture of the new Australia. Only the people in the Wade area of my story can and may retain the hunting and wandering skills of the last century.

By the turn of the century, south of Perth, the churches had established missions for remnants of the tribes almost extinguished. North to the Gascoyne, the West Australian coastal tribes had been working on stations with little cohesive tribal organisation. From Broome north, the incursion of Chinese and other pearl divers had left a complex of coloured races which had little of the old Aboriginal tribal organisation left. Far north in Queensland and the Northern Territory, tribal groups persisted with some indication that their law and ways of life would persist. This is now changing. As always, there has been Malay influence along the coast, the country being tropical. White incursion here has not disrupted tribal life as much as elsewhere. This, as I have said, left the great sandy deserts of the centre as the last stronghold of the indigenous tribes. It was time for a Bill Wade to protect them. The clearly defined tribal areas preserved those tribes outside boundaries where the treatment of the white invaders had decimated the people and destroyed their oral culture preserved over thousands of years.

But it has been the breakdown of the totem system that has harmed the real culture of the Aboriginal people everywhere. The totem system of marriage probably took centuries to develop. Once broken, as it has now been in most areas of Australia, it is irrevocably destroyed.

It could be said that the Aborigines were themselves guilty of dispossessing previous owners of the land; I think not. The bones of great predators still preserved on the salt shores of Lake Callabonna indicate that Australia was the home of the great carnivorous creatures long dead but, in terms of earth's age, quite recent. It is likely the present indigenous peoples, although speaking different tongues, were all escapees from an ice age that followed the lush period when coal was formed. Nothing dating so far back remains to indicate an Aboriginal ancestor predating this era. I have seen those great bones on Callabonna; they were shown to me by a half-caste tribesman who stood in awe of the Dreamtime. The power of the unknown, past and present, whispered by pretenders to divination, is stronger than any other bonds.

You may make mock pretence to freedom but the thrall is there.

I bless Wade for his open skies religion, a forgiving Father God, a dying Saviour paying a price. No mystery. His arms held wide in welcome to every living soul. Promise for the dead. Wade's religion needed no walls, no water, and no baptism — it was perfect for the naked, unlettered children of the great dry sandy deserts.

It is hard to believe that the European settler who invaded this continent had a social conscience of the sort which seems to be developing now that the occupation of Australia is complete. How foolish to believe 'that honour's voice can now provoke the silent dead'. What nonsense to believe that generations can carry the guilt of history. What can be done is to relieve the frustration of those confined to ghettos who pine for the privacy of freedom which can never be achieved in the atmosphere of prison-like settlements, unwittingly provided by missions, now controlled by state and federal governments. I do not mean freedom to own city centres or deforested lands, these would be another straitjacket. Rather, it would be better to show those who are able, a way to join the multicultural community that is Australia. None could eulogise a wage-slave way of life, but there are ways, many ways, for those who pick their path through the modern jungles, though they long for the old ways, the vast distances, an uncluttered world.

'Ernabella'

On his second journey from Beltana going north, the explorer Ernest Giles made a brave attempt to find the remains of his old mate, Alf Gibson, the man lost the previous trip far west of the Musgraves. Giles never found any tracks or trace of the lost horse or rider. In memory of his companion, he named that vast wilderness the Gibson Desert. The journey north from the Everard Ranges to the Musgraves crosses a desolate spinifex region. Giles arrived at a creek he had called the Glen Ferdinand on his previous trip. The plain at the eastern end of the approach to the Glen Ferdinand, with its permanent spring`— that years later became the site of 'Ernabella' — Giles eulogised as the nearest thing to paradise. The explorer wrote in his diary:

> *In all my wanderings over thousands of miles of Australia I never saw a more delightful or fanciful region than this and one indeed where a white man might live and be happy.*

Years after our journeys, I told old Stan Ferguson about this 'delightful place' and he left his home at 'Moorilyanna' and took up 'Ernabella' and built a stone cottage which is probably still there.

Far out from all cilivisation, many days' camel journeys from 'Ernabella', by camp fires and lonely hills, I had watched Wade singing to the eager naked native children, this self-appointed teacher, this un-nominated priest without cassock or surplice. Watching him work, I knew then and I know now that the Father of Jesus Christ was the God of all peoples, all creeds, one with the mountains, the storm and all creation, calling all the people of earth.

'Come unto me,' Jesus said. 'I am in the Father and the Father is in me.' Is this a new religion? I think not, but a better one, and more easily understood.

When the naked man picked up his spears and clutched his spear-thrower (woomera) in one hand, with the other hand pointing his direction for the day's travel to his family, all he owned of value was in one hand. How uncomplicated! He looked to the wind; always hunting upwind. The direction of the breeze would dictate the way he went, for animals live by the scent of everything about them.

If we were going west and the wind was blowing from the east, the local tribe would not follow us. Sometimes we would wait for a headwind for it was usual to allow the Aborigines to go along with us as much as possible for, all along the way, the young people would chatter about the game, the local area, the bushes, the water; always the water.

Nothing on earth is more elementary than a tribe of native, naked people who own only the land and all that nature provides — nothing else. Each day these proud warriors strode out from their bare camp fire abode, sufficient in the arrogance of their ability to meet the day's needs. Behind them came their long-suffering wives, also empty-handed, on their heads bearing the wooden bowl and digging stick, leading or carrying the children of the tribe. At the end of the day, the men might bring to camp a kangaroo or an emu, but invariably the women would have a few fat grubs, or a dish of winnowed seed, or even a yam dug from deep down in the desert soil. It is the women who fight the hardest for the family life and, of course, life itself.

To and fro across the sandy wastes we went, unmolested. No doubt the smoky telegraph had said:

They are harmless, our women are not molested.
When we shake a spear they smile and pat us on the back.
When they look for water we are not punished to tell them
of our hidden waters; they sit down and wait for rain.

When we are sick they help.

One man is mad but he has a new corroboree religion about a man in the sky which will make a dance. The children are learning to sing.

And so Wade and I walked the land in peace and became one with it.

Meeting Treloar

Our first water after leaving the station country had been at the place that would become 'Ernabella'. To our knowledge, few whites other than Giles had ever set eyes on the waters of 'Ernabella', although there were always a few men, born to wander, who walked alone into the wilderness before explorers, before settlement, ahead of all recorded travellers.

One such was Arthur Treloar.

It was a dark night; stars lit the sand bed of the creek where I had unloaded the camels — a foolish place to risk a flood, which often comes out of the far distance to drown the unwary, but this I had yet to see.

I noticed a light blinking mysteriously far up the sands. Was it a star low down? Hostile blacks? The elusive min min? I had to know!

The sands of the creek bed make their own peculiar squeak if a hasty foot disturbs them, not loud, but a wary listening ear can hear it. I walked slowly, placing each foot carefully down, hunting the light that still blinked small and lonely in the distance.

A tent, a tiny tent. Inside, a kerosene lamp swung from the pole, an old man, grey bearded, sat reading.

I called to alert my presence.

'Treloar,' he said.

Even stranger than it was for me, must have been Treloar's shock at seeing a white boy hundreds of miles from the nearest settler.

It was a strange and lonely meeting in the night. His camp fire was cold, out.

The night was warm and very quiet.

This is the story he told.

In the second half of the nineteenth century, before the railway stretched to Oodanadatta, the head of the rail line extending from Adelaide to the north had been at Maree. From there, all goods went north by camel pack or by bullock wagon.

Speaking slowly and softly, as men who have lived their lives alone in the desert speak, Treloar said, 'I left Maree with a bullock wagon, one bull and a few cows, and rations for a year or more, looking for a place to settle. There were no settlers north of the line head and few white men had seen what lay beyond the line.

'When I reached the wide sandy river they now call the Alberga, I had gone far enough. I camped on a water hole and dug a shallow well, it was a good season.

'There I stayed breeding up my cattle. Every year I made the long trip down to Maree for rations; flour, salt, bullets, there was not much else I could afford. The little money I had came from people travelling north who bought beef from me.

'Years later drought came and wiped me out. I walked away without even a horse to carry my swag. I went south and married, but now I come back here, where I belong, to peace.'

I was to meet Treloar once again. He had not stayed alone in the Musgrave Ranges area for long. He had returned to Oodnadatta where he had a place north of there called 'Eringa', and from there eventually to Adelaide where he ended his days in the old men's home at Magill.

Forty years later, by chance, a piece of paper came to my notice with the word 'Umberatena' on the letterhead, reminding me of another wandering journey where I had

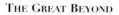

called, for a drink of water, at a place so named and owned by a man called Treloar. I wrote, asking if it could possibly be that one of his ancestors was the pioneer of 'Eringa', the man I had met in 1926 at 'Ernabella'.

The answer came: 'It was.'

I am tempted to include the extraordinary story of this great old pioneer. But it is a drama that needs a book of its own to illuminate the story of one of Australia's great individuals.

The Glen Ferdinand plain can certainly be very special. In 1926, crossing it from the east, we came on another most unusual character. He was alone, no horses, no swag, no rifle, just a black billy can which he said he used to make tea from the heart of the tchilga bush. For food, his only source was a flock of two thousand sheep.

'Wandered up from New South Wales,' he said, 'came up the back way.' This, you will agree, is an original pioneer. There were some native women and children far out in front of the sheep. It occurred to me that his flock would diminish fast once he made tucker bag friends with the tribes. When we met, he had as yet not made contact with the real Myall blacks. This was the year when the desert blossomed.

The Great Beyond

As I mentioned earlier, crossing the lush, flowering Glen Ferdinand plain in 1926 had been an unforgettable experience; a vast panorama of colour. According to his diary, the year Giles saw it must also have been such a year.

To reach the big mountains that were the Musgrave Ranges, crossing the trackless unknown and drinking at the lonely waters was for Wade and I the end of our first step into the western deserts, and the beginning of the great beyond — our entrance to the sandy deserts. It was quiet there under the big gums, just the far-out hills and a dingo yapping his loneliness to the listening stars.

The eastern end of the Musgrave Ranges was almost the unknown except, as I have said, to a few hardy bushmen who 'fared out alone to their unknown lands'. To us, who had not yet read Giles' or Warburton's diaries, it was the gateway to the Great Sandy, the Gibson, the Great Victoria deserts. We had not yet seen or met a naked tribesman, although their leaf shelters, camp fires and artefacts such as discarded weapons were everywhere about the 'Ernabella' waters. We also did not know then that we were camping on one of the very few permanent waters in that vast western land. Light rain had kept us camped at 'Ernabella' for several weeks — and tribesmen and women came to see the intruders.

The bulk of the Musgrave Ranges, which rise to five thousand odd feet, runs west from the 'Ernabella' water. The Glen Ferdinand Creek on which we were camped runs north–south. Our old friend, Treloar, could not tell us what lay beyond, except that tribesmen he'd met had spoken of a big rock hole, somewhere on the south of the ranges.

We went south.

The Musgraves rise sheer out of the flat plain. One can step off the flat plain onto a rock and, in one place, climb five thousand eight hundred feet to the top — all rock. Looking south from the top of the range is like looking into infinity, except to the south-east where rises another set of peaks showing as a smudge on the horizon. All these distant peaks were destinations to Wade and there were many of them in the million square miles we were to travel. This is not to say that we investigated them all, but we did a lot in the next year or so. The peaks that rose like sentinels in the Great Victoria Desert were granite, like the Musgraves, the Deering Hills, the Warburton, the Everard, the Mann ranges, and that alluring finger pointing into the great Gibson Desert: the Petermanns.

After the massive rock called Mount Woodroffe, which rises three times the height of Ayers Rock, we were not so impressed with The Rock as perhaps are those who have not had the fortune to see Woodroffe. No wonder the Aborigines were so keen to keep that group of desert ranges for themselves. Now, after Wade made his plea to the government, the Aborigines again own that mighty group of rocks, and others may only enter with special permit.

The usual method of a day's hunt for a family or a group of families consists of all women, youths and dogs going slowly to the windward end of an area, while the men slowly comb the country from the night camp into the wind, thus driving the kangaroos or wallabies into the waiting dogs and those men delegated to help the women. This method of hunting would soon destroy the native game if it were not for the constant shifting of all humans from place to place. Imagine, if you can, a family alone in a wilderness of desert; no shops, no refrigerator, no hospitals, no one to help in time of trouble — alone. Naked, without reserves of food of any kind. These people of the wild must be more fitted to survive than any except, perhaps, the Eskimo.

One ability the Aborigines of the central deserts have, which others lack, is that mysterious ability to communicate. Smoke signals are hardly sufficient to account for news that seemed to be available concerning happenings among other members of the tribe, sometimes far away.

The one piece of vital intelligence which we so often asked, was about the waters. The young men could tell about waters far out in the desert, but never how much water or how big the supply, or how deep the well.

Most of the explorers of the 1800s had some botanical knowledge but the exigencies of the trips they made invariably precluded any carrying of specimens or even examining and recording the flora of that vast conglomeration of deserts and mountain ranges.

Wade was in no hurry, so that even without any botanical training it was possible for us to note the trees, the bushes, the flowers and to give them names as that knowledge came to us in later years.

The desert oak which grows on the flat lands between the ranges is the outstanding tree of the desert. A close relation to the she-oak of the northern pastoral country, it also looks similar to the river oak of Queensland. Forests of this useful desert tree are a relief from the monotony of the spinifex and sand.

The trees that dominate the southern Victoria Desert are the mallee gum, small clumpy trees that grow close together with numerous branches all near the ground. At times there is water to be got from their shallow roots.

Where there are creeks, the eucalyptus red gum sometimes occur, even in the far-out sandy deserts.

The mulga and gidgee of the pastoral area are not a feature of either the central Gibson or Great Victoria deserts but the mulga seems to flourish in the far western Victoria Desert edges.

Pituri, the supposedly localised plant of the river, does grow in the Deering Hills and on the south Mann Ranges. Not a tree as some have written, it is a bush almost the same as tobacco. (There is a tree, which the Aborigines called tchilga, which is a narcotic.) The ashes of this shrub-like pituri form the base of the pituri drug used by all western Aboriginal tribes.

The plug of ashes and pituri are common to all the tribes of the western deserts. After being chewed, the plug is a white masticated mass about the size of a large marble carried in a bunch of hair tied up at the back of the head or behind the ear.

The chief locations where the pituri grows are the granite hills of the ranges in the boundary corner where South Australia, the Northern Territory and Western Australia meet. Also, I have noticed it growing along the creeks which flow into the northern side of Lake Eyre and, most particularly, the rocky outcrops of the creeks flowing from the Simpson Desert side of the Georgina River.

Pituri could have been the currency of trade used by the tribes of the areas where it grows, for I do not know of any area elsewhere that this particular weed is found.

Chapter 5

Explorers

To be set afoot five hundred
miles or more from
the nearest settlement
might not be fatal for me,
but ... would be a serious
prospect for Bill.

The Explorers

When Sir Thomas Elder and the West Australian Government imported camels to Australia, it was principally for the purpose of exploration. Elder personally outfitted several explorers to look at the country beyond his holding at Beltana, north of Adelaide, a place on the edge of the dry country (on the north–south telegraph line which ran from Adelaide to Darwin). Elder's prime objective was to explore a possible overland route for cattle from South Australia to Perth.

Speaking at a farewell dinner given in his honour at Perth Town Hall in 1899, the explorer David Carnegie, in the presence of West Australian Premier Sir John Forrest and the State Surveyor-General Mr Johnston made the following observations about the area:

> *I regret that I am only able to give such a bad report of the far interior of this colony; but even so, and even though it has not been our fortune to discover any country useful to the pastoralist or miner, yet I hope we have done good service in proving the nature of a large tract of country previously unknown.*
>
> *Such an expedition might be undertaken for pleasure; but this I should not recommend. Few countries present such difficulties of travel or such monitory of scenery or occupation.*

Sir John Forrest, who crossed through the worst possible country in the million square miles of desert Australia in 1870, gave a similar report on the country between Beltana in South Australia and Kalgoorlie in Western Australia.

P. E. Warburton, who made a crossing in 1875, was fortunate in seeing slightly better range country, but his report on the journey was still of a desolate and useless land.

Strange though it might seem to readers of these pages, my impression — though not coloured by comparison with other more lush countries, as were our explorers of last century — was to feel an empathy with the whole wide land.

Perhaps this was because Bill Wade and I were not rushing desperately through the area and so were able to spend more time than the explorers experiencing rain and dry storms and calm times, the flowering of desert plants and the raging bushfires, followed by the greening of the eremophilas. I had all the excitement of watching these and of living with stone-age youths my own age. There was everything there to colour my love for the dry lands which has never left me, and I know that Wade felt the same. He proved his love for the desert and its people by living the rest of his life in service to his dreams.

Colonel P. E. Warburton C.M.G. was perhaps unfortunate in selecting his route from Alice Springs north to the Oakover area of Western Australia in 1872, a most difficult traverse to attempt as a hurried journey. His report, given to his sponsors Elder and Hughes, was even more dismal than that from any of the others who followed.

The 1870s was a decade of journeys from South Australia to Perth via the desert interior. Beginning in 1869, the Forrest brothers, John and Alexander, had made historic explorations following a route north of that made by Edward John Eyre in 1884. Sir Charles Nicholson, who chronicled the early expedition of Forrest in 1869, wrote that:

... vast areas of the interior still remain untrodden by Europeans is an undoubted fact.

It may, I think, be reasonably assumed that the whole interior region, west of the 140th degree of east longitude and north of the 30th degree of south latitude, is of the most unpromising kind.

Eyre, Giles, the Forrest brothers, Warburton and others made a determined dash across these lands. All agreed in their diaries and documented reports that the country was a desert land. It remained for Wade to live —and love — and to spend the rest of his life at Warburton in this wilderness; it was a place of great isolation, beautiful in its splendid undisturbed peace and naturalness — rugged, primitive, magnificent. Now it remains the place of the Aboriginal tribes who called it home.

Those who have lived long in the barrens may laugh at the extremities experienced by those who came to this land from softer climates. I quote Warburton:

The number of flies in Australia and the rapidity with which they breed are quite horrible: They assail the ears, nostrils and eyes of the traveller.

The ants prevent our having a moment's rest, day or night, and we don't know how or where to escape them.

Sturt turned back when he reached the 'stony desert' — still so named. Later this same stony desert became the grazing grounds for the stock of our pioneer cattlemen. It is now held in lease by the son of a great Australian bushman, Billy Brooks, who took up those stony lands after others failed.

Old Artie Rowlands, who spent seventy years in Sturt's Stony Desert country caring for cattle, said of it: 'It was my country.' He loved it. I do not deprecate the heroic suffering and courage of those brave men who explored. I simply point out that they were not 'of the land' as are the Aborigines, or as are those who followed the explorers, those who spent their lives building a nation — our pioneers.

It is important for anyone reading these lines to know that in 1926 there was no means of communication west of Oodnadatta. An understanding of such vast distances would enable readers to better comprehend the problems of communication. The country from the end of the rail which ran from Adelaide to Oodnadatta had been taken up in the late eighteenth century, some near the rail as early as the 1870s, while the farthest selections were not established until much before the Wade journey.

One of the members of the Carnegie expedition which had crossed the same path that we were on only thirty-two years before was Joe Breaden, who had taken up country eighty miles from our starting point at Oodnadatta. Joe had bred horses on the Alberga River at a place he called 'Todmordon'. He had sold it to a man called Young who was still the owner when we passed through. It was here that Paddy DeConlay and Victor Dumas were working in 1926, when we first met them. Breaden must have still held an interest after he sold 'Todmordon' because Molly Breaden, Joe's daughter, took it up again in the 1950s. Joe Breaden played a major role in the Carnegie expedition of 1894–95. His name should rate high among the truly great explorers of desert Australia.

Another name which should rate high, if not as the most impressive explorer who crossed the deserts of the country between Alice Springs and Western Australia, was Ernest Giles. Giles made his historic trips twenty years before David Carnegie. Both crossed through the flat-topped Alfred and Marie Range, although they did not agree on the locality

which, as I have indicated before, was the reason previous explorers hurrying through there had made varying positions for the waters they met. And this is probably the reason Alfred Gibson was never found when he left Giles to go back to their camp. Gibson's death is one of the mysteries of the exploration era of Australia. I have met old bushmen who claimed to have found the Strezelecki death camp, but no one has found Gibson's remains. It is a big country.

On September 30th, 1872, P. E. Warburton recorded in his diary:

Just before reaching the lake, we had captured a young native woman. This was considered a great triumph of art, as the blacks all avoided us as though we had been plague stricken. We kept her a close prisoner intending that she should point out the native wells to us; but while we were camped today the creature escaped from us by gnawing through a thick hair rope with which she was fastened to a tree.

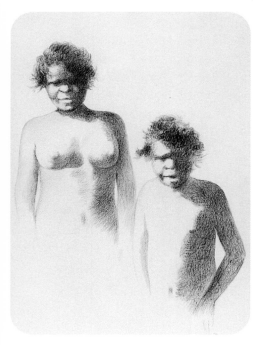

Imagine the utterly humbling humiliation of a tribal woman who is shy and modest.

Explorers who went there treating the Aborigines as lesser people — unlike Wade — deserved the fate which repaid them for their attitude to the people of the desert tribe. The surviving few from this long ago episode have told me why their tribe refused to help the intruders.

Can you wonder why a few of the western desert people were so fearful of Wade, until they adopted the 'halabelula' man? And again, can you wonder how Wade was able to live in these inhospitable regions for a lifetime, wandering at will, guided by the friendly inhabitants after his acceptance.

Down in the southern Victoria Desert area, Wade and I met people who remembered what had happened when they were young, back when their people met various explorers in the 1870s. The men at Ullaring would have been little more than sixty years old when we met them, and they were men with fierce memories. These were among the very people that Wade embraced as brothers and whose hearts he won.

Warburton continues his account:

Had it been otherwise not one of us could possibly have escaped their spears — all would certainly have been killed, for there were over a hundred of the enemy, and they approached us in a solid phalanx of five or six rows, each row consisting of eighteen or twenty warriors. This was the best organised and most disciplined aboriginal force I ever saw. They must have thoroughly digested their plan of attack, and sent not only quiet and inoffensive spies into the camp, but a pretty little girl also, to lull any suspicions of their evil intentions we might have entertained. Once during the day the little girl sat down by me and began a most serious discourse in her own language, and as she warmed with her subject she got up, gesticulated and imitated the action of natives throwing spears, pointed toward the natives' camp, stamped her foot on the ground close to me, and was no doubt informing me of the intended onslaught of the tribe.

The Future

Having seen and praised the remarkable adaptation of the desert tribes to an environment so demonstrably harsh, it might be allowed that a comment on the future of all Aboriginal people would assist in explaining the present furore about the part that they, as an indigenous people, may play in the future of Australia. Those people, who are now living in such settlements as 'Ernabella', 'Docker River' and Warburton were, and still are, the tribal people. Those six hundred and forty million wild acres are their own to wander and they can, if they wish, continue to enjoy a migratory life similar perhaps to the Tauregs of northern Africa, the Ebos of Nigeria or the outer Mongolian shepherd peoples. If they do not adapt to the self-supporting status of such other desert-living peoples then the alternative is adoption into modern civilisation. Those who are now living in cities or country towns have no alternative but to become citizens of Australia and adopt work habits, otherwise they will need to be fed and clothed. They cannot go back to a stone-age way of living, it would be impossible. The exception, as I have stated, might be a few desert people who have maintained the ability to hunt and survive.

When water in dams or wells is provided throughout those vast areas of the Aboriginal reserves, permanent date plantations could make self-contained depots so that migratory tribes would be able to live off the land as other peoples of desert countries have done for centuries. However, the populations will never be numerous. Unless food is supplied by white governments, this artificial condition cannot be a permanent solution to maintaining a healthy Aboriginal lifestyle. Nor would those vocal descendants of several races with Aboriginal blood — now thinly watered by cross-breeding — want to adopt Aboriginal customs.

Traditional customs included the splitting of the penis to avoid overpopulating and the mutilation of the women for the same purpose. Death was the sentence for breaking community law, such as the taking of a wife of a wrong totem in tribal breeding practice. Would they want to face the secret kadaicha killers who walk at night, or the pointing of the bone by a dubious law maker? I think not. No! These people have not the wish or ability to regress to the old ways. Nor are many content to join the struggle for existence which non-Aboriginal people suffer.

It is just not possible to go on feeding and clothing a minority who will not try to adjust. They, as others, must join the eternal battle of existence or, as the alternative, become itinerant hunters like their forefathers in that vast land which is still their own. That or become itinerant herdsmen living off the flesh and milk of their herds as do the migrating peoples of the northern African deserts.

I suggest that there are now two entirely differing peoples calling themselves indigenous: those who might live off the land, and those who want a complete integration into the Australian peoples. Many of this second group have already become good cultured citizens.

The Future of Indigenous People

The peoples of the northern coast, such as those of Arnhem Land, have a much simpler way of living an organised tribal life because of the ease with which food can be grown or fish can be used as a staple diet. My prediction is that if the Aborigines, who want to adopt European ways, do not soon adapt to this way of life and occupy all the coastal areas west of Darwin, then others — who are already used to living off tropical land — will take it over and will, in time, fill it with many millions of other peoples.

The rivers which run into our northern waters are highly productive. There are flood plains which can be drained and cultivated, river flats that can be irrigated and vast waters such as the Argyle Dam, which is a source of great potential wealth. All these waters are envied by the crowded Asians.

For the desert tribes, the methods of population control might seem to be cruel, harsh or primeval, but those who know the dry inland can appreciate the systems of control which the inhabitants of early Australia adopted. By this I allude to birth control, which was so vital to the continuity of a maximum population that any area could carry.

The evidence that the old were simply left to die is beyond question. In about August 1927, we came upon a lonely old woman with a baby in her arms. She was in the last stages of hunger and thirst. The child did not have much evidence of life, but it was not dead. Tracks around the camp indicated that no one had been close for several days. The pair had been left to die. Giles recorded a similar circumstance of the old being left to die.

I will diverge from my story to record another trip through the area from Giles' records.

GILES' DIARY (1872)
FROM THE GIBSON DESERT

Our supper was spread, by chance or Providential interference, a little earlier than usual. Mr. Young, having finished his meal first, had risen from his seat. I happened to be the last at the festive board. In walking towards the place where his bedding was spread upon the rocks, he saw close to him, but above on the main rock and at about the level of his eyes, two unarmed natives making signs to the two quiet and inoffensive ones that were in the camp, and instantaneously after he saw the front rank of a grand and imposing army approaching, guided by the two scouts in advance. I had not much time to notice them in detail, but I could see that these warriors were painted, feathered, and armed to the teeth with spears, clubs, and other weapons, and that they were ready for instant action. Mr. Young gave the alarm, and we had only just time to seize our firearms when the whole army was upon us. Taken by surprise, their otherwise exceedingly well-organised attack, owing to a slight change in our supper-hour, was a little too late, and our fire caused a great commotion and wavering in their legion's ordered line. One of the quiet and inoffensive spies in the camp, as soon as he saw me jump up and prepare for action, ran and jumped on me, put his arms round my neck to prevent my firing, and though we could not get a word of English out of him previously, when he did this, he called out, clinging on to me, with his hand on my throat, "Don't, don't!" I don't know if I swore, but I suppose I must, as I was turned away from the thick array with most extreme disgust. I couldn't disengage myself; I couldn't attend to the main army, for I had to turn my

*attention entirely to this infernal encumbrance; all I could
do was to yell out "Fire! fire for our lives." I intended to
give the spy a taste of my rifle first, but in consequence of
his being in such close quarters to me, and my holding my
rifle with one hand, while I endeavoured to free myself with
the other, I could not pull the muzzle at my assailant.*

These were the people Wade was sent to meet, tribes whose
only contact with white people had been hostile. Had these
tribesmen wished to kill Wade, they could easily have done
so, as he would never have taken firearms against them. His
approach was always an open arms, friendly way — which
they seemed to sense — and he was never molested.

At times the tribesmen of the Mann Ranges were inclined
to show signs of antagonism to white man's intrusion but
never as an outright attack.

Routine

Our usual day was a routine of repeating the monotony of
walking into new country. To keep them from straying, all the
camels were hobbled on the front legs while we were in camp.
When they were released after a day's journey it was my job to
unload the camels, fix the hobbles, take off the nose lines,
check the bells on their necks and release the clangers on the
bells which were silenced during work. Reversing the process
in the morning, I would roll my swag, listen for the bells, then
set out with a bundle of nose lines over my shoulder and head
for the sound. Sometimes, not often, the bells were too far
away to hear. This meant circling the camp for tracks, locating
the direction the camels had taken then, like a human blood
hound, running the tracks as fast as I could because the
camels would be walking, especially if we had a dry camp and
they were thirsty.

It is a fear that sets the heart beating when one knows that
one's life is involved with the finding of the team. To be set
afoot five hundred miles or more from the nearest settlement

might not be fatal for me, but living off the land, bare-handed, would be a serious prospect for Bill.

Only once did I seriously doubt whether I could catch the wandering camels. That time they had made a determined attempt to cross the desert patch between the Musgrave and Mann ranges. It seems from the diaries of desert travellers that such a loss has been the fate of many cameleers.

Wade would point the direction if we were attempting to go south into the Great Victoria Desert — which we often probed from the Musgrave, the Mann or Tomkinson ranges — or west from the Rawlinsons, north or north-east from the Petermann Ranges.

There was unlimited scope for wandering in those areas without attempting to go north from the big rock or wander in that impossible scrub above the Nullarbor.

The finding of water was easy if the local tribespeople were with us, for they knew every soak or rock hole. To them, the land was a book with many pages which had stories kept in tribal lore for centuries; with them, it was a delight to see the treasures of the desert revealed.

When it became apparent that Wade was determined to cross that frighteningly empty desert between Latitude Hill and Mount Margaret which has swallowed up good men, I suspected and later confirmed that Wade was determined to conquer the complete crossing — either to prepare for a permanent stay in the tribal lands or to replenish supplies at the goldfields. He did both, for his eyes were on the Rawlinson waters, which is where, later, he lived out his life.

We crossed easily over the rest of the Great Victoria Desert, and passed Gibson's mysterious death sands. Like a homing pigeon, Wade never hesitated until he reached Mount Margaret Mission, near Laverton, which was run by Rod Schenk and his wife Mysie. They had a couple called Reichenback, also missionaries, living close by them.

I had gone around the circle — Laverton, Kalgoorlie, Adelaide, Oodnadatta, Laverton — thousands of miles, and

Dowey ps 136:25

was due to go again, for my travels and Wade's had just begun. Next we were to go back into the Gibson Desert, then return to Oodnadatta, across a thousand miles of native lands.

Somewhere on our hurried dash across what was to become Wade's future supply route, we must have passed Akbar Khan and his bride for they arrived at Mount Margaret Mission not many days after us.

Akbar brought in his half-caste girl, Lali, from the west. She had red hair. He told me he had bought the girl from her mother, a woman of the Willorara tribe, a woman who had been 'bushed' by a white man, west of Oodnadattta. Because the Willorara people moved across a vast area and were a sparse tribe living in poor country, I could not identify the exact spot where he had found this girl living with her mother and the family tribe. And besides, at that time, I had little knowledge of the geography of that vast area from the Great Victoria Desert to South Australia. In fact, at that time and at that young age, I had little knowledge of anything and so I did not then appreciate the significance of Akbar's situation.

When Akbar and Lali arrived at Mount Margaret, she was barefoot and naked except for a short shirt, and he was clad in shorts only.

Wade and I had travelled with camels, water cans and supplies of food. Akbar had none of these. But he did have Lali as companion, which would have enabled him to live off the land.

There are grubs in the trees, frogs in the claypans, rabbits, goannas, birds — all food to the people who are trained from birth to use what they find.

Akbar's story of his purchase of Lali, their escape from the angry tribesmen, their journey across the desert, and what happened to them at Mount Magaret is worth telling. It was, and is, an epic journey.

Chapter 6

At Opperinina

*I was ... quietly lifting
my head to peer at
what was coming,
when I looked into the
face of the turbaned hunter
who had climbed from
the opposite side.*

The Journey Continues

The first winter was almost over. It had not been unduly harsh, there had been general rain allowing us to travel far and wide, meeting the scattered peoples of the deserts, people who gather only on rare occasions when there is plenty of water and grass for game.

All tribal business is done at these gatherings; marriages arranged, penalties imposed, judgements made, great singing, dancing, lovemaking. We had seen one such gathering which could have been one of the last great gatherings of its kind before white settlement affected the Aboriginal nation's power structure.

The families were scattered as they were in good seasons; growing lads were allocated to their tribal teachers to prepare them for the battles of life. Old people were delegated to the easier rather than the cruel, demanding sparser areas. Some old women, too fragile for the long treks, were left to die.

As was our custom, we retreated from the harsh lands of the north-west and south-west to spell our camels in the confines of Opperinina water. Sheltering high hills screened the more fertile valleys near the springs. There was wood and water, and game was in the hills in abundance.

Ayers Rock was visible in its towering splendour from the high hills where we made a depot. The depot was merely a log structure with a frame, where heavy unused things could be left for shelter — which was important in times of rain or storm.

Mystical stories surrounded almost every valley and rock. Do not discount these tales, probably handed down from the time of the great lizards, a time when Aborigines were much the same as they are now — or at least as they were in 1927, when the old men of the tribe still held the traditions of the ancient people. Not even the most primitive cavemen could have been more basic spear hunters than the men and women we lived with in the desert. Their only history was the memory of that which had passed by word of mouth since man first battled the great predators.

The tales of the prehistoric animals, told by these age-old people who have carried the stories by word of mouth, could well be the only records now available, and these soon will be lost. Those tribes of the deserts were still living as they had for millennia when Wade met them as a friend and talked with them on that basis.

A few places still held so much dread that no tribesman would dare visit them. One such was a water hole in very rugged country where a reptile of immense size was supposed to live. That had probably been ten thousand years ago or more, but the fear still lived on.

It is possible that poison gas, escaping from subterranean fires, made some places taboo. Also the death of a tribal hero made his place where he died into a sacred place. All these stories became the talking points in those times when no other communication existed.

It is most likely that the desert Aborigines we were talking to, a people who had no contact with other worlds for thousands of years, and who spoke of terrible birds which fly, were telling stories about carnivorous lizard-like birds which our museums have reproduced from skeletons. Stories upon stories were repeated over the centuries until fable became fact and truth an uncertain myth.

We have it ourselves, not about animals, but about the unknowable in the Book of Genesis.

Looking across the fire, listening to the old men teaching the young ones, the thought came to me that 'this was home'. They had no other — no old folks' home, no other shelter from the storm. Take from them the camp fire and the water hole and all that was left would be death, which is no doubt what happened to the Derie people of the Cooper River and the Birdsville Track.

Bells in the Night

In 1927, Opperinina, so close to Ayers Rock, was almost unknown. None of the explorers had mentioned seeing this useful water, which was hidden deep in the ranges.

It had been a year of silence. Now, at Opperinina on the western end of the Musgraves, we were surprised to hear the clanging of a travelling camel team. (The bells strapped

to the neck of the camels, muted for travel, would be released at night. By day they could be heard as a dull clanging while the camels rolled along.)

Here was a long string of gaily decked camels and colourful native women in long bright dresses. There was one white man, Ted Coulthard, who was accompanied by a tall, dark, turbaned camel driver.

Coulthard was as surprised as we were to see a white man's camp. The long line of newcomers circled the water before moving away to a place where wood and clear ground made another suitable camp. When fires were lit and his camp arranged, Coulthard came across to our camp.

'I am heading for the big water the Aborigines talk about. Opperinina. Is this it?' he asked.

We were — or at the least I was — glad to meet a fellow to talk with. Wade was a great prayer man, however he was not a great conversationalist. After several months together, he had talked himself out. I guess he was lonely, too.

But, to him Coulthard was a sinner to be saved and so Wade worked on him.

The camel man who was with Coulthard went hunting, and I went hunting, and we met on the rocky cliffs where wallabies abounded. He had a .22 Savage, a new, powerful, long-cartridge rifle which made my old Remington a relic. I know that the old side-delivery Remington was the gun that won the American West, but it was not in the same class as the high-velocity Savage. Together, we sat on the peak of the rocks looking down at the plain.

'See that rock,' he said. It was a half mile away on the foot of the range. He raised dust close by that faraway rock with his high-powered rifle and this amazed me.

'I am just temporary with Coulthard,' he said. 'I will go north from here.'

This was my first meeting with Akbar Khan. Next time I met him was far away at Mount Margaret. But at this stage, at Opperinina, Lali — the naked tribeswoman he had purchased — was in hiding, and Akbar did not want to disclose her presence to us or any of the tribesmen who might be about, for the couple had already broken tribal rules and were therefore in danger.

Wade and I left Opperinina before Coulthard. The tall camel man also left when we did — we were going west, and he was headed out towards the big rock which later became known as Ayers Rock. He did not tell me why, uttering just a casual phrase, 'I'm leaving.'

I noticed that he had little to carry when he left — no swag, only a rifle and a small bundle of flour and some sugar that we had given him. Some men travel light but he was almost barehanded, though he did have the best gun ever I had seen.

Akbar was lean and hard. Not all his colour was sunburn. He was a tribesman from a faraway country, a Baluchi, from Indian places that Wade knew of but of which in those days I had never heard.

After leaving Opperinina, Wade and I crossed to the Mann Ranges thence down into the Great Victoria Desert and when we reached the western edge of that desert we estimated that it would be possible to visit Mount Margaret Mission in the Western Australian goldfields area to collect fresh supplies.

It was while we were at Mount Margaret that the man Akbar and his girl arrived, having travelled the barren lands of the Victoria Desert. He still carried his rifle, still wore the tattered short trousers and he had a bundle of dog scalps which he hoped to trade at the mission. With him was a girl who, he later told me, had walked the whole distance from their South Australian meeting place.

Akbar and Lali were still empty-handed, except that Akbar had the bundle of dog scalps that he had collected. They were worth two pounds each, which was a lot of money in those days.

Lali was pregnant so the mission took her in charge, and advised the local Aboriginal protector, who later collected Lali and shipped her off to Moore River, the Aboriginal settlement for coloured girls.

Akbar was angry, very angry.

To earn some money, he sold his scalps and bought an old truck with which he traded meat with the mining camps.

Leaving Wade in Mount Margaret, I went with him on one of these trips. We camped together on that hot night near Lake Carey, a goldmine that was booming at the time, was our destination.

During the journey Akbar told me what had happened before and after we had met him at Opperinina.

Lali was his, he said. He had bought and paid for her.

Akbar did not like the Christian mission which had taken his woman from him. He had been born a Mohammedan. He could not explain why he believed as he did. But he surely knew that he should pray five times a day. Bill Wade, who had never come across a Mohammedan before, liked that idea, but for a man to worship blindly seemed to him to be a neglect of 'the way'.

The Lord is my strength and my redeemer.

This, to Bill, was a far better idea, for he believed that redeemer meant redemption — a free gift, a forgiveness (though he never, even in his confiding moments, would go into the finer details of his own need for forgiveness). Saved, to Bill, was saved, forgiven, redeemed, born again, a new start, a being held in the everlasting arms — all because Jesus had said so.

His was a great acceptance. Looking back, I can confess to having lived in the shadow of a few great men and Bill Wade was one of them. Millions have lived and died in the Christian religion without accepting the total offer that their Christ made clear:

He (or she) that believes in me. I will come in and sup with him (or her) and they with me.

It's bedrock stuff. But I don't think Akbar wavered, or even listened.

He was like the Buddhist priests who chant blindly 'Omdahum', or the millions who cry 'Allah is great' in a hopeless hope. They don't open their hearts and souls to an acceptance of an offer to walk in companionship day by day with the Christian God through.

All this Christianity was foreign to Akbar. His simple religion consisted of 'Allah is great' repeated five times a day. He understood nothing more.

A desert-bred man, Akbar was older than I. His face was wrinkled and burned — the colour of polished teak. On his head he wore a turban, with its tasselled end falling over one shoulder.

Men of his breed do not often speak, and they seldom confide. It was a year after I had met Akbar at Opperinina, that I became trapped with him on a lonely bush road near Lake Carey in his broken-down truck. It was a night, after a scorching day, that still held the temperature past the century at midnight. We knew where the nearest water lay, but experience had taught us that one does not survive long walking in that heat. We decided to take our chance to correct the silent engine in daylight.

We had little in common that would encourage talk between us except the brief encounter at Opperinina in the Gibson Desert a year before, about which I have written.

The scattered hills in the central Australian desert areas, where we'd hunted, are granite peaks that form sheltering caves and watersheds which act as harbours for wallabies and euro kangaroos. At their base, water collects in the sandy soils acting as storage. These soakages are the life source of wandering Aboriginal people.

I was climbing such a rocky peak, alert for a shot at one of those rare rock wallabies, quietly lifting my head to peer at what was coming, when I looked into the face of the turbaned hunter who had climbed from the opposite side.

We were some miles from the Coulthard–Wade camps when we looked into each other's faces across the rocky peak. Both of us expected to see a rock wallaby. It was a strange meeting. And it was stranger still that on this night, a year later, I should hear his dramatic tale.

We had parted, not expecting ever to meet again. Opperinina was a very lonely place, the nearest settlement several hundred miles away. He did not explain his presence there then, when my curiosity led me to ask. Although we had never met before that startling confrontation on the desert mountain, our paths had crossed many times. We discovered we both knew the camel drivers of the track leading from Oodnadatta. And he had worked briefly at cattle stations among people I also knew.

Akbar's Afghan people were not my people but almost, as if by adoption, I felt akin with them in that sparse land where people's lives were not secret and where one man's struggles were the survival experience of them all. There was so much in common.

I drove camels and that also was the sole occupation of the Afghans. When the Afghan knelt on his mat to pray to Allah, I believed there must be one God over us all. My early teaching fell away. I was kin to the Afghan and I learned to despise the priest or parson who called the Mohammedan 'heathen'.

Akbar Tells His Story

That was the background of the man who sat with me on that fearsome hot summer night as we waited anxiously for daylight and what it might bring.

I asked him: 'The day you hunted, when we met in the desert, were you alone?'

Akbar did not speak and seemed to have some kind of a hesitation to answer. Then, as though the floodgates opened, he began a tale which seemed incredible.

'You will remember,' he said, 'that I was carrying a high-powered Savage rifle. Well, that was my sole possession, except a knife which I always carry in my belt.

'When we met, I was alone. But my woman was a tribes girl who I had bought from her mother. She was still naked and I had no way or wish to clothe her. So, for reasons you will understand, I did not tell you about her, nor ask you to meet her.

'Nor,' said he, 'did I know at the time just where she was.'

That night, camped by the broken down truck, the tale Akbar Khan told me had all the evidence of truth, for I knew the places and people of which he spoke. Nor could his words be doubted, for he spoke as a man in deep passionate trouble, without reservation or attempt to deceive.

Only that week, I had been present when Akbar's girl had been taken from him into the custody of the State. Now she would be far away where he could not hope to see her again. The man I was listening to was a troubled, unhappy man.

The night had cooled little from the extreme heat of the day. We were both suffering.

'You cannot understand our religion. We are not bound by the Christian beliefs which hide the true nature of a man,' Akbar said. 'We are what Allah has made us, to know and acknowledge that we need a woman. And in his wisdom, Mohammed gave his people that freedom to take what women a man can rightly afford to keep and care for. You Christians hide your true nature behind a curtain of beliefs.'

In defence of my people's long-held Christian faith, I said, 'Do you believe that Mohammed was greater than the Jew, Jesus?'

Akbar was silent for a moment, then he replied, 'Mohammed wrote:

If the world had been prepared to listen to Jesus there would have been no need for me to have spoken.

There we sat waiting for the daylight in order to fix that old truck. It was only thirty miles or more to the mining camp but we knew that once that burning sun came up, we would both perish before we reached water.

Akbar was a different man to the half-naked savage I had thought him to be when he sat with me on the granite peak overlooking Opperinina a year before. Barefoot, clad only in a pair of ragged shorts and his battered turban and clutching his precious rifle, I had taken him to be a Ghan gone native. Not so. There, on that rugged peak, he had not spoken of himself.

Akbar, who sat out the hot night by Lake Carey with me, showed himself to be a man of resource; a practised camel driver, a Mohammedan of strong beliefs, a very determined man. The desert is a harsh master, a place for survivors. Akbar had shown that he could live with it, but the road ahead was to be much harder.

Neither of us could have imagined what the coming years would involve. But, for the moment, he was an angry man ready to do violence — anything to get his girl back. The police had taken her away and he, lacking knowledge of the laws of Australian Aboriginal departments, could not fight. He was desperate. For minutes at a time, he would be silent, sitting there in the darkness.

Determined to survive and keep his girl, Akbar had been peddling meat to the miners and hawking other small, needed things while he waited for his girl to have his child.

Tonight, in the truck, he was carrying fresh meat which, in a few hours, might go bad. No doubt he was worried about that, too. He could not afford the loss of a whole load of fresh meat.

He talked about his woman as we sat there and no doubt he wondered if he would ever see her again. Possibly it helped him to talk, for he knew that, like himself, I had lived in the desert, and we were somehow akin.

Akbar began by explaining to me how he had come to be in the desert.

'I was camped with old Mick O'Donough, who had been breeding half-caste kids for years, some of them grown now to working age. Others had lived and worked about the station and had likewise bred sons and daughters with the Aboriginal women.

'Being an Afghan and, like all my people, shy of white women, I thought there might be a few half-caste girls who might marry me in my religious way which was what I wanted. My people all agreed that one or two, perhaps up to four girls, would be allowed by my creed, but for now I wanted one. Mick told me of one girl who had been born to a woman of the Willorara tribe after she had left his area. The story he had heard was that the girl had red hair and no tribesman was game to claim her for a bride because of some superstition which they had.

'Mick said, "Why don't you take a few bags of flour and sugar, that should buy the girl from the tribe. A few sticks of tobacco and a tomahawk would be sure to get her. That is, unless she takes fright of you and clears out".'

Akbar said, 'That's just what I did. Old Mick O'Donough sold me the stores in exchange for a few dog scalps which I had. That plus a couple more camels to carry the load, and I left Mick and went west into the desert.'

The desert west of 'Granite Downs' was almost an unknown area when Akbar set out in search of his girl in 1925. A few explorers had crossed it; some had died. Most of those who hurried across the thousand miles of scrub, spinifex and sand had been scared of the blacks and had shot at them, thus creating bad feeling among the tribesmen. The area had been named the Great Victoria Desert back in the last century. None of it was known in detail except that it was dry, desolate country, inhabited by hostile people.

'I was scared,' Akbar said.

The Great Victoria Desert runs for almost a thousand miles from 'Granite Downs' through to the goldfields of West Australia. Looking for a small group of wandering people in that wilderness was a frightening prospect.

'And I was alone,' he added.

The night wore on, it was too hot to sleep. Neither of us had brought swags. We had reckoned that the distance to the mining camp at Lake Carey was such that we could have delivered the load and been back to Mount Margaret, my base, hours before this.

'How did you find the tribe in that wide area of western lands?' I asked.

I had noticed Akbar seemed reluctant to tell the rest of his search for a bride.

But he continued: 'After I crossed the Everard Ranges, the country was sand ridges and spinifex, then into a scrub of small mallee gum trees so close together that the loads on the camels tended to bash their way through the branches, which made it necessary to stop and sew new corners on the flour bags every few hours.

'Ahead, a single peak mountain showed on the horizon. That is where I made for, as it is usual to find a soakage at the base of those granite hills. There was a native well at the foot of the big rocky slope, which made me decide to use this hill as a base to explore the country for a hundred miles each way to see if any tribespeople were in the area.

'I was fearful that the people in this desert would take me for a white man and spear me before I could get to know them. I am not white and with my black beard I might have been accepted as another tribesman. That is what I hoped.

'Eager as I was to find my red-headed part-Aboriginal girl, it never occurred to me that she would not understand my language nor would I be able to speak to her. But I knew that her mother must have been east into the station country, even though her visit might not have been for long.'

Akbar was silent for a while, then continued: 'Far to the south, a smoke showed on the desert. There were people in the area. I camped and waited, in turn making a smoky fire each day. The mystery of an unusual smoke would attract attention from a wide area and could even bring warriors of the whole tribe to inspect an intruder. As I learned later from my bride, the people of the ancient desert tribes speak to each other by a language which has no known transmission among more educated peoples of the world.

'Even she, in some degree, had the ability to hear this unspoken language of the mind. Her degree of this ancient mysterious cult grew lesser as the years went by, but there were never secrets that her mind could not penetrate.'

Akbar continued his story in bursts of words that were almost incomprehensible as he thought back to the lonely ride he had made looking for his woman — who had been then just a dream.

'Many times, footprints of wandering tribesmen led me to follow their direction but the tracks were always made by huntsmen, and I was fearful of being speared from ambush,' said Akbar.

'Then, near a southern lone mountain, I met women and children. I gave them some sugar, something they had never tasted, and this made me friends with them, especially the children.

'First a child, a naked tousle-headed boy, showed his inquisitive head among the bushes. I knew it was by design, not accident. He was sent to test the situation. No doubt, I had already been watched, observed, assessed. It would be known that I had a rifle, much flour, tobacco, and that I was alone.

'Men came, spears no doubt close by, but hidden. It was a peace deputation.

'Not one of the visitors could speak English, hardly necessary when all that was needed was a hand out with tobacco. We traded smiles which was enough and they silently vanished into the bushes.

'I thought it wise to saddle up, and indicated my intention to travel. A leader, the oldest of the bunch, pointed me to go south which I felt would be the way they wanted to go, carrying my great wealth, which no doubt they hoped to share.

'So south we went, watering at their hidden waters, and for ten days we walked.

'The destination was a deep rock pool hidden in a granite outcrop, no doubt a permanent water. The tribe — women, children, old men — all were there, a sort of reception committee. Among them was a woman who spoke a little English and, with a shock, I saw the red–gold girl, so different. Naked — yes, but shapely, shy as a hunted animal, aloof, separate, a jewel in a strange primitive setting.'

Chapter 7

Akbar Khan's Story

There, on that dusty road to Lake Carey, came to me the light which has never failed me since, that the Christ of the Cross belonged to all.

Buying a Bride

'*I*t was my turn to show no interest in the girl or any female,' Akbar said. In those desert places every look, every glance, every action of a stranger is assessed by people who read the signs of life by their ability to judge the climate, to hear, see, observe and survive.

He continued: 'I was among a superior people, those who had never known a book or a building, but could live where few, very few, of the educated, civilised cultured people could survive. Such was the superior wisdom of theirs, another world.

'Making camp far out from the water, where my camels and I would be, caused no interference with the tribal life. I built a fire, set up a ring of packs to give some privacy, stowed the precious flour under canvas, hobbled out the camels and waited.

'Nothing happened that day nor the next. Men hunted, women carried water, children played. At night a rhythmic chant, almost music, came from the camp. I did not visit nor show an interest.

'On the third day, young men came holding spears, pointing me to the distant hills and patting my rifle — an invitation to hunt.

'I was afraid to leave my camp unprotected but the invitation was pressing.

'We walked single file. I am tall, trail hardened, and I can walk, but I was no match for the youths who, through generations, and whose forefathers for thousands of years, have known no other transport but walking.

'Along the way one would divert to spear a wallaby, a rat, a bilby in the hiding recess of the spinifex. It was a wonder to watch.

'My Afghan people are known to be the ruthless hunters of the mountains of Afghanistan, a nation of survivors. But nothing before or since has been so evident of the fact that the young men of the Great Victoria Desert are matchless in their abilities.

'When the sun was high we stopped on a flat rock where a covered pit held water from the last rain. Two boys set to work making fire; a crack in a dry log was filled with dry kangaroo dung with the hard edge of a spear thrower. The two boys sawed fiercely across the crack, dropping hot carbon into the dung, which began smoking.

'This was placed on a handful of dry grass and waved to and fro until it flared. We had fire. Cooking, to hungry young Aboriginal spearmen, is a very quick, almost unnecessary, affair. It consisted of laying the gutted animals on the fire until the hair was burned off the unskinned carcass. The not-so-nice-looking dish was torn apart by eager teeth until the bones were picked.

'There is no pantry or store room or refrigerator in the tribesman's camp; breakfast time comes when the hunt provides, sometimes not at all.

'Civilisation begins with plentiful food available, water and storage — none of this exists in the dry deserts where only water is the fundamental factor.

'My first day with a hunting-for-survival party of stone-age men was a memorable one. Every moment is clear in my memory. For instance, a kangaroo is sighted in the distance, and hands behind the back with fingers working tell

me to tread quietly, be still, come! It's a language which is universal, almost a primitive instinct.

'I learned much that day.'

As Akbar talked, I thought of similar times when I had hunted with the boys I'd known.

However, now it was time for him to tell of his mission there — to buy the red-haired girl who was to be his woman.

'Bargaining for a bride is not easy when the ownership of the girl is a tribal affair and the mother is not a seller, nor the girl available to be sold,' he explained.

'I started on the old men who, not aware of what I was buying, took the bribes of flour and tobacco without knowing what my intentions were.

'There was no stopping the trade now. The flour and sugar soon went, leaving me a taker rather than a giver, for I was no match for the hunters. I decided to leave and reluctantly headed back to the station country to purchase more trade. Bride-price goods, but this time I would be more careful. The trouble was I had no money. Dog scalps were the only source of cash available. The South Australian Government bounty was seven shillings and sixpence for a dog or a pup scalp.

'I hunted, trapped and poisoned as I went. Dogs were plentiful, bringing enough money when I crossed the Alberga River into station country to buy me a full load of trade. This lot had to be a bride-price, but first I had again to find the tribe, a needle-in-a-haystack job. A million square miles of desert Aboriginal tribal country where they wandered at will, although localised, of course, by tribal boundaries.

'I would find them.

'First I went back to where I had left the family who owned my girl. About another month, at least, for I could not go direct to the hill where the contact had been made. Then I followed my own tracks with the wandering tribe. No good trying to cut their migration tracks, my skills were not that developed.

'The camp fires were cold and dead. The tribe and my girl were long gone, but their last tracks were plain in the sandy hills of the Great Victoria.

'I was like a bloodhound spurred on by a great longing. I would find her!

'Day by day, the tracks led to camp after camp, all on small waters. Her footprint was in my mind now. It would be there when they left each camp. Some days I would pass the night, stop and walk on, often making a wide circle to see which way the old folk had gone, eliminating the hunters' tracks. The tracks wandered, sometimes almost too windblown to see. A week, a month, always in the same direction now; far ahead a tall blue range showed that that would be the destination.

'I thought the ranges were outside tribal boundary but could not be sure as my knowledge of the language was very limited.

'Leaving the tracks which I had been following, thinking to gain on them instead of wandering as the tribe had done in search of food, heading now for the tall peak which seemed to be their objective, I made an almost fatal mistake.

'Not expecting to meet hostile tribesmen it came as a shock when a spear, coming out of trees as I passed, missed me by a miracle. Turning to look at my camels, the spear had shaved my back. I leaped sideways, dodging the next spear. Looking for the enemy or — what could be more than one — I saw at a glance that the spearman was alone and without more spears. Perhaps I should have tried to make friends at once. Instead, in anger, I leaped towards him as, for the instant, he seemed astonished that his second spear also had missed. Grasping him by the waist, I kicked his feet from under him. I fell on his naked body, knocking the wind out of him. Too surprised to move, he looked up at me and, realising my mistake, I smiled and held out his spear-thrower which had fallen as he fell.

'Was it the smile, or the gesture of returning the woomera? I cannot tell. Perhaps it shows that even in the heart of the wildest stone-age men there is response to a smile.

'No doubt the tribal people I had been following were moving north into other people's territory, which is what I learned later from my girl. My girl! Sometimes I despaired of ever seeing her again. It seems that there was to be a great meeting of tribes in the Musgrave Ranges and, for the time, all hostile action between the tribes had ceased while the conference was held.'

Akbar believed that his girl had lived her life in fear of being killed because she was a half-caste. Although she had not been initiated, being protected by her mother in that isolated family, her time would have come. She would have been claimed as a wife or consort by some old man of the tribe and then killed if she had refused. This fear had probably made her flee at the first opportunity that came.

It was at this point that I stopped Akbar in his tale to tell him that Bill Wade and I had actually seen this great gathering, and this meant that we had, at that time, been travelling very close to him.

As Akbar's tale progressed, I realised that he and his girl had never been more than a few miles distant from us until we finally met Akbar at Opperinina, and he was alone then.

It was a mistake on my part interrupting Akbar. Always a solemn, reticent man, he did not take up his story again until, after searching in the cabin of his old truck, he came over with two lemons — something which has remained in my memory, for that was a terribly thirsty night.

He continued: 'Seeing that there were many camp fire smokes ahead where the plain met the Musgrave mountain, I went west and found a rock hole to water my camels and make a camp.

'The tribespeople found me within a few hours and no doubt circulated the story of the tall strange dark man. This information brought a visitor, my old tribesman, the head of the group with which my redhead lived.

'The big conference of tribes lasted several days, after which the people I had been tracking came to my camp. I had at last found my girl.

'No doubt the remembrance of the flour, sugar and tobacco sticks was the thing that brought them. I was happy to hand out more of the bride-price, which is what I believed was the thing to do.

'I knew some words — such as man, woman, boy, girl, water, kangaroo, mine, yours, gun, spear.

'These helped, for I was anxious to trade for my redhead and be on my way.

'This was not to be so. The mother and her people seemed to accept the things I gave them as purchase price for my redhead, but she would not even look my way. Kept aloof from her, I must have looked strange with my turban on my head and tattered short trousers and boots, all so different from the lithe naked boys of her tribe who perhaps had been her standard of manly beauty. No doubt they had told her my indication of trading the treasures to the tribe in exchange for her.

'We had shifted south into the sandy desert to a rock hole where there were wild figs and ripe quandongs. It was a good camp but I wanted my woman. By now I reckoned that the price was high enough and had been paid.

'Evidently my redhead thought differently and took fright. She left the family in the night, her tracks showed going east along the range, a strange extraordinary thing for a girl to do except perhaps that no humans on earth are so self-supporting as the desert-bred Aborigine.'

The Chase

'The older men of the family offered to hunt the girl and bring her back. This hurt my pride for, by now, my desert experience was making me feel equal to the desert-bred locals which, of course, I was not.

'Leaving my camels, my swag, my tools, everything except my rifle, my belt and knife, and wearing only my short tattered trousers and my turban, I set out to track down my bought-and-paid-for bride.

'She had almost a day start. She must have been terribly afraid. Lacking a detailed knowledge of the territory her people had visited in attending the great corroboree in the Musgraves, she made her first, almost fatal, mistake. She travelled the creek which erupted from the Musgrave Ranges, following its sandy bed into the depth of the big hills. Further and deeper into the range she went, her tracks easily followed. She did not know it, but where the gap led was forbidden ground. She had broken the fatal taboo which governs all females of the tribe.

'I also did not know that this was sacred ground until a warrior stopped me with a spear poised to throw.

'Involuntarily, I raised my loaded rifle and, from the hip, fired.

'With a yell, my opponent dropped his spear and woomera and fled. The bullet had not seriously harmed him.

I could not see what damage had been done but it had certainly frightened him.

'Entering the well-trodden circle of a recently used ceremonial ground, I realised what a terrible mistake my girl had made. She also would know by now and she would be quaking with fear, but fear lends wings to the feet. Her tracks showed that even with my long stride it would be hard to track and catch her.

'The gorge was narrow, in places just wide enough for a man single file. The sides of the mountain were steep, rising out of the creek bed. It was unlikely she would attempt to leave the bottom of the pass.

'Water — she would have to find water — and as her tracks showed, she had diverged in flight to look at possible rock holes for a drink.

'I estimated that the gorge running through the mountain pass was twenty miles. Neither of us would know what lay beyond the pass through the mountains.

'By now my redhead must have taken thought of where her flight would lead her. She was like a bird let out of a cage that would fly until it had no strength to go further. This I reckoned on and expected that her need for food would stop her flight.

'The male members believe that they are the saviours of the tribe. This is not so. It is the women who dig the rabbits, search for grubs, grind the seed for bread, dig the yams, burrow for the honey ant.

'From birth the girls become matchless trackers and providers. My redhead was a tribal girl. She would survive. The question was: would she ever relent and allow me, the pursuer, to find her? I hoped she would.

'This could be a long, hard chase. It was my turn to look for water and hunt for food.

'Far up on the granite slopes I heard a spearman cry. He had seen me and was alerting the tribe. The smokes would

alert a nation of desert people that the taboo had been broken — "Kill! Hunt! Destroy the woman! Trap the intruder!" the smoke would be saying.

'My rifle is a .22 high-powered Savage, a long, powerful cartridge, the first and the best of its kind. I took careful aim at the rock the hunter stood upon when he cried the alert. The shot scattered chips over him. It was too far away to hear his cry but no doubt he would have uttered a cry. At least the enemy knew the risk they took. I hurried on.

'Night would be a terror for my lonely redhead. I walked and ran until dark when there was no light to see. I made no fire and sat hunched, cold in a shallow cave.

'The gorge was still narrow. When the full moon came up I hurried on. Today I would catch her.

'What then? Would such a wild thing submit? Was that what I wanted? No. There must be some way, when we faced the common enemy who would no doubt kill us both, that perhaps her fears might allow her to see me as a way, a friend. If she had noticed the way I treated her tribe when first we met, might I not become an ally? Who knows what a woman thinks?

'Morning came and with it the risk that every rock, every corner, might hide a pursuing tribe of stone-age fierce avengers.

'Was she already dead?

'Her tracks led out away from the mountains, north to the surrounding desert. I found where my redhead had cooked a rabbit. She had, like all her people, carried fire in a hollow stick, precious fire for women do not have the hardened woomera to make fire for themselves. But she had not left me a leg or a bone. I was desperately hungry.

'At noon, her tracks led to a long high rocky ridge. She could be hiding there.

'I would wait, make a fire, hope.'

Akbar spoke as a man of the mountains. 'We live with

hope but also fear. Those other inbred terrors — hunger, thirst, cold — added to my fear as they must have to that lonely child ahead. She, for all her stone-age breeding, shared those life-destroying fears. She had lived within the shelter of the law, protected by ever-available food and shelter. Let that flimsy cloak vanish for a single day, and the destruction of all the covering shelter of civilisation will leave us as naked as were our cavemen forefathers.

'My redhead and I were alone, desperate, hunted, cold and fearful. It was just possible that those fears might turn her to me as a deliverer, for surely she had judged me with searching eyes when I played with the tribal children. Then she did not seem to notice me, but no doubt she had heard gossip of my intentions which, because she was a maiden, had helped create the fear which made her flee.

'I walked around the rocky outcrop looking for tracks leaving the hill. There were none. At the southern end of the rocks, the fresh track of a warrior, left only minutes before, gave me a chill. Every moment I expected to hear a shrill scream, the death cry of my redhead. Keeping out of sight as much as possible, with gun loaded and prepared to kill if I had a sighting of the native hunter, this took me an hour. She had to be hiding. No doubt she would know now that I was hunting not her, but her elected killer.

'Would she accept me as her protector? There was no choice, if only she would let me know where she was in those rocks. I could see neither her nor the hunter. Both had been trained all their lives to disappear, fade into the local cover. Choosing the west side, with the sun at my back, I waited for a sight of a fleeing girl or a stalking spearman.

'Night came on. I knew now that this was what she was waiting for. I stayed, silently expecting either my girl or the rustle of the hunter and the singing spear. There was a late moon. When she came, it was silently. As stealthily as a prowling fox, with a raised hand she pointed out into the spinifex desert, showing me how to hide my footsteps by stepping from spinifex bush to the next bush. It would delay any chase.

'We walked the night through without a word until we were on the edge of a shallow lake, a salt lake, deep enough to hide our footsteps. When I stumbled, she reached for my hand. It was forgiveness, acceptance. No night would be too long, no pursuit too terrible. She, my girl, was with me.

'On the far north-west side of the lake, we followed a shallow water, a fresh creek. There we stopped. Her firestick was gone but I had the meroo, the spear-thrower, left by the man who had tried to kill me. Soon we had fire in a deep sheltering bank of the creek. We lay exhausted, no thought of anything but rest. By that fire we slept. When the sun rose, she had found freshwater mussels, and had caught a rabbit by the simple method of moving in a circle around its squat, circling, picking up the animal alive.

'We ate, she searching the horizon for smoke or a sign of pursuit. There was none.

'The problem for me, having won my girl, was where to go. East, I knew, were stations. None of the white men there I would trust with my naked girl, who I was careful not to frighten with amorous advances. Both of us were satisfied just to be alive. Both of us knew that we were to be killed on sight. But we were content. Lali, for that was her name, was adopting me more by the hour, getting food was fun, staying alive was a wonderful thing.

'To go south to her people was risking the skills of the most skilful hunters on earth. They were also very organised; we were even careful about our thoughts, for the power of thought is the telegraph understood by primitive people. To go west was an unknown way. Hills showed on the western horizon, the granite hills, those age-old rocks which have pitted holes where water stays. North we could see the great rock, a place my redhead knew from tribal gossip to be a gathering for many tribes.

It was not often used by the people of the fierce mountain men but, in using those waters at its base, we would have to leave tracks when moving on.

'We started west and had gone not a half-day when, across the plain, were fresh camel tracks,' Akbar said.

Listening to his story, I assured him they were not Wade's and mine. There would have to be many camels in that place, driven or ridden by white men who wore boots. The procession was not more than a day ahead, he said, because the camel dung was fresh.

Akbar said, 'Such a caravan would have flour, sugar, perhaps rice. I had nothing to trade. Most men, I knew, would accept the company of my redhead for a night as trade. That was not for me, then, or ever. I would die before any other man ever touched her. The problem was if we stayed, soon our enemies would find us. But to hide without food was to starve.

'Lali told me by signs that we should separate. She would go stealthily north to the big rock. The watering place was easily found. Old leaf shelters and camp fires were everywhere. An emu had been plucked and cooked, leaving a pile of feathers. Lali pounced on these, quietly making for herself a pair of the feather slippers which leave no trail. Clever girl, she had twisted the gut of two rabbits, dried them over the fire and with a bone from the rabbit leg made her rough but  effective boots. She indicated that when she reached the big rock she would drink but leave no tracks.'

Akbar indicated to the girl that he would see what the white men might give him, then follow her north.

From Ayers Rock, for this is the area where Akbar and his girl separated, to Opperinina Spring is a long two days' walk. As Akbar continued his tale of that lonely crossing through the spinifex, I could imagine the fiery brush rubbing against his hurrying legs in places where the prickly spinifex grew thick.

'So you found Coulthard and asked for flour — what did he say?' I asked, reminding Akbar again that this was the time we also had first met.

Akbar said, 'Coulthard was four hundred miles west of his nearest supply base, and flour was scarce. He told me, "All our supplies are precious."'

Akbar left Coulthard, anxious to find Lali, who he knew would be hiding at the rock waiting.

On the morning of the second day, Akbar approached the rock which looms out of the desert like a great cathedral. He told me he dared not approach without scouting for fear of what might happen. With a loaded gun and hiding behind every shelter, listening, and watching for smoke, he examined the ground for tracks, his girl's or any other's.

'Slowly I got near the rock,' Akbar said. 'On the southern end of that huge lonely rock there is a soakage. A few small caves with old camp fires told me that here was water. She would be waiting, watching — but how to let her know I was there? We had not learned enough of each other's speech to arrange a signal. That came later when we had both practised the curlew cry which served us well. But for now, I had to think of a way to find her. Barefoot, I crept up to the face of the rock, leaving my footprints which she would know. And she did.'

Again I interrupted him, for there was hesitation in his voice as if he were about to tell me of a passionate reunion.

'Do you hate these people who are so keen to see you both dead?' I asked.

The harsh lines of that hard face softened. 'No, I cannot blame them for resenting the intrusion into their age-old customs, the invasion of their sacred places. When I first met them they treated me well. It is I who was to blame.'

The red-haired Aboriginal girl whom Akbar loved had become a woman. Now it was time to mate because the urge of passion cannot be suppressed, and the mother instinct in woman is the strongest force in humans.

Akbar almost smiled at this stage of his story and I knew that somewhere at the rock, in a sandy cave or corner, Akbar and Lali had mated and would never again be parted.

He continued the story. 'We could not stay at the rock. The desert around it holds tracks that are too hard to hide. The rock is just a single slab where hiding for long would be impossible. To the west, we could see more huge rock.

'Placing our feet on the prickly spinifex, we left little sign of the way we went. This would not stop a hunter for long, but by then we hoped to be far away.

'The way west brought us shelter in a great jumble of granite boulders which also would hide our steps against possible hunters who might be lurking behind us. There were no tracks here, which gave us the confidence to risk lighting a fire. Our night together at the big rock had made us eager to gamble on stopping to camp together again. We knew now we were in love.'

At this point in his tale, Akbar's voice broke and his head bowed. I saw a strong man — used to silence in his lonely life and at one with his God, Allah — broken.

'Allah is great.' He repeated it. Then gently, in almost a whisper, he said, 'She is gone. The police have taken her away. We are not like your people. We are another colour, we have another God. Allah is great.'

I could have wept with him then, for it came as a great revelation that my people have neglected those of whom Christ said:

Other sheep have I which are not of this fold.

There, on that dusty road to Lake Carey, came to me the

light which has never failed me since, that the Christ of the Cross belonged to all — black, yellow, or white; Pathen, Muhammedan, Hindu or heathen. Too much distinction has been made by un-Christian-like men.

'We will get your girl back,' I said to Akbar. 'The police, who have taken her to the half-caste home at Moore River, cannot keep her in chains. You must go, like you fought for her before, and steal her back. She is yours!'

And we did.

Although Lali had found people of her mother's totem at Mount Margaret, which meant she had sisters, brothers and tribal relations, she never lost her fear of being an alien. A mother is a mother in all tribes, but totems are related, which meant Lali had many relatives — no doubt her story was already known there.

Fifty years after the night when Akbar told me the tale of his purchase of Lali, and of their adventures, I received a letter from Mona, their eldest child. She had a sister and two brothers and Lali had told them that I would be the only person left alive who had known Akbar and herself at Mount Margaret and would be able to tell the story of her life.

Mona asked, could I . . . would I . . . perhaps write to her? She was living in Bendigo. After a second letter came with the same request, I did set about writing Akbar's story for her.

My letter was never finished, but I did call and tell her a little of the drama of her mother, of how Akbar and I planned the abduction of Lali from Moore River and I helped get them married and settled at Renmark, South Australia.

Lately another request has come from the grandchildren of Akbar and Lali for the same story. It is a story of great courage: how Akbar bought and paid for Lali and fled with her across the wastelands of the desert to Mount Margaret. Akbar is now buried in the graveyard in lot number 62 — at Renmark, South Australia. Lali, as an old woman, fled back to look for her people who, after half a century, were no

longer there. She is buried in an unmarked grave close to her mother's people. The ties of childhood are strong.

Akbar never relaxed into his people's traditional ways of keeping women. And his old friends, including the one who buried him, told me that Akbar always kept Lali in secret isolation, as was the custom of his Muhammedan people, even in Renmark where they lived, where there were other people of alien culture.

Perhaps for this reason, after her children grew up, Lali longed for the talk and the voices of her people who, by then, were scattered and mostly dead.

Those who lived in the goldfields had adopted white men's ways. The totem system had no longer any power. I think of her, in those last years of life, as if on a sad mission, seeking a world that had disappeared.

Chapter 8

Uneasy Progress

*I watched in wonder
as Wade put his arms
about the painted leader,
speaking the only word
for 'welcome friend'
he knew —'Yemeragee'*

Lali's People

*T*he eastern Victoria Desert people, who were Lali's people, came from as far east as the Musgraves and drifted west to Mount Margaret and Laverton on the northern end of the West Australian goldfields. My evidence for this is the people I met at the large corroboree held in 1927 in the Musgrave Ranges, at the edge of the desert country. I could speak some of their language and a few could speak a little English.

I saw them again a thousand miles west at a later gathering. That gave me the evidence that the real desert tribes were able to wander over a large area without infringing other tribal boundaries.

Other evidence of the huge areas that the Pitjantjara tribes used is in a story written by David Carnegie in his diary when he made a dash from Kalgoorlie to Halls Creek and back through the Petermann Ranges.

Carnegie wrote:

We noticed how kind they were to the poor diseased buck, giving him little tit-bits of half raw rat's flesh, which he greatly preferred to any food we offered him. They were strange, primitive people, and yet kind and grateful. We anointed the sick man's wounds with tar and oil (a mixture used for mange in camels), and were well rewarded for our unsavoury task by his doglike looks of satisfaction and thanks. We had ample opportunity to watch them at night, as our well-sinking operations kept us up. They seemed afraid to sleep or lie down, and remained crouching together in their little hollows in the sand until morning. To break the force of the wind, which blew rather chilly, they had set up the usual spinifex fence, and between each little hollow a small fire burnt.

In exchange for numerous articles they gave us, we attached coins round their necks, and on a small round plate, which I cut out of a meat-tin, I stamped my initial and the date, C. 1896. This I fixed on a light nickel chain and hung round the neck of the good-looking young gin, to her intense gratification. It will be interesting to know if ever this ornament is seen again. I only hope some envious tribesman will not be tempted to knock the poor thing on the head to possess himself of this shining necklace.

Amongst their treasures which they carried, wrapped up in bundles of bark and hair, one of the most curious was a pearl oyster-shell, which was worn by the buck as a sporran. Now this shell (which I have in my possession) could only have come from the coast, a distance of nearly five hundred miles, and must have been passed from hand to hand, and from tribe to tribe. Other articles they had which I suppose were similarly traded for, viz., an old iron tent-peg, the lid of a tin matchbox, and a part of the ironwork of a saddle on which the stirrup-leathers hang. This piece of iron was stamped A1; this, I fear, is hardly a sufficient clue from which to trace its origin. Their weapons consisted of spears, barbed and plain, brought to a sharp or broad point; woomeras, throwing-sticks, and boomerangs of several shapes, also a bundle of fire-making implements, consisting of two sticks about two feet long, the one hard and pointed, the other softer, and near one end a round hollow, into which the hard point fits. By giving a rapid rotary movement to the hard stick held upright between the palms of the hands, a spark will before long be generated in the hole in the other stick, which is kept in place on the ground by the feet. By blowing on the spark, a little piece of dried grass, stuck in a nick in the edge of the hollow, will be set alight and the fire obtained.

As a matter of fact this method is not often used, since, when travelling from camp to camp, a firestick or burning brand is carried and replaced when nearly consumed. The gins sometimes carry two of these, one in front and one behind, the flames pointing inwards; and with a baby sitting straddle-legs over their neck and a cooliman under their arms make quite a pretty picture.

Amongst the ornaments and decorations were several sporrans of curious manufacture. Some were made up of tassels formed of the tufts of booby's tails; other tassels were made from narrow strips of dog's skin (with the hair left on) wound round short sticks; others were made in a similar way, of what we conjecture to be bullocks hair. All the tassels were hung on string of opossum or human hair, and two neat articles were fashioned by stringing together red beans* set in spinifex gum, and other seeds from trees growing in a more Northerly latitude. This again shows their trading habits. Here, too, were portmanteaus, holding carved sticks of various shapes and patterns, emu-plumes, nose-bones and nose-sticks, plaited bands of hair string, and numerous other odds and ends.

These quotations from his diary would indicate that David Carnegie was a kindly man. He further apologises for such behaviour, as the following quote from his diary indicates:

Those who judge me cruel in my treatment of the aborigines may never have faced the exigencies of death from thirst and starvation.

The previous extract from the diary continues:

After a long, tedious day of tracking, we found ourselves back at our own camp. The natives — two bucks, two gins, and three piccaninnies — travelled North to a dry well, and there split, the men going one way, the rest another. We chose the bucks to follow, and presently the rest joined in, and the whole family swung round until close to our camp. We could, by their tracks, see where they had herded together in fear under a beef-wood tree not one hundred yards from us. Just before sunset we again set forth, taking Czar and Satan as riding-camels, and were lucky in picking up tracks going in a fresh direction before night fell.

We camped on the tracks and ran them in the morning, noticing two interesting things on the way: the first several, wooden sticks on which were skewered dried fruits, not unlike gooseberries; these were hidden in a bush and are remarkable, for they not only show that the native have some forethought, but that they trade in edible goods as well as in weapons and ornaments. These fruits are from the Solanum Sodomeum, and were only seen by us near the Sturt Creek (three hundred miles away). The second, little heaps of the roots of a tree[1] stacked together, which had been sucked for water; we tried some, but without result, and the tree the natives had made use of did not seem to be different from others of its kind. This showed us, too, that they must be dry, and probably had had no water since our arrival at their well. About midday we rode right on to their camp without warning. Again the scrub befriended

---

* *beans of Erythrina*

[1] *known to me as pine-mulga*

them, but in spite of this I could have got ahead of them on Satan, had his nose-line not snapped. Determined not to be baulked, I jumped down and gave chase, old Czar lumbering along behind, and Warri shouting with glee and excitement, 'Chase 'em—we catch 'em,' as if we were going through all this trouble for pleasure. Happy Warri! he never seemed to see gravity in anything. It is almost incredible how quickly and completely a black-fellow can disappear; as if in a moment the whole family was out of sight. One black spot remained visible, and on it centred my energies. Quickly over-hauling, I overtook it, and found it to be an old and pitiful gin, who, poor thing! had stopped behind to pick up some dingo puppies.

Nevertheless water was there, and thankful I was to find it, even to drink it as it was. After half an hour's work in this stinking pit, I was sick from the combination of smells.

I decided to take the gin back with us, as it had been clear to me for some time past that without the aid of natives we could not hope to find water. With our small caravan it was impossible to push on and trust to chance, or hope to reach the settled country still nearly five hundred miles ahead in a bee-line. Even supposing the camels could do this enormous stage, it was beyond our power to carry sufficient water for ourselves. The country might improve or might get worse; in such weather as we now experienced, no camel could go for more than a few days without water. I felt myself justified, therefore, in unceremoniously making captives from what wandering tribes we might fall in with. And in light of after events I say unhesitatingly that, without having done so, and without having to a small extent used rough treatment to some natives so caught, we could not by any possibility have succeeded in crossing the desert, and should not only have lost our own lives, but possibly those of others who would have made search for us after. 'A man arms himself where his armour is weakest,' so I have read; that, however, is not my case. I am not justifying myself to myself, or defending a line of action not yet assailed. I write this in answer to some who have unfavourably criticised my methods, and to those I would say, 'Put yourselves in our position, and when sitting in a comfortable armchair at home, in the centre of civilisation, do not, you who have never known want or suffered hardship, be so ready to judge others who, hundreds of miles from their fellow-men, threatened every day with possible death from thirst, were doing their best to lay bare the hidden secrets of an unknown region, as arid and desolate as any the world can show.'

I had no time to observe for latitude at this spot, the position of which is fixed merely by dead reckoning. The rock-hole lies eight miles from it to the S. E. by E., and has no guide whatever to its situation. I christened the well 'Patience Well,' and I think it was well named.

D. W. C
1896

These quotations from the diaries of explorers of unquestioned bravery and merit show the difference between Wade the man who came to stay — he lived and died there — and those hurrying through a country which was never to be their home.

Far be it for me to judge that Carnegie, Warburton, and others who braved these barren lands were not Christian in their beliefs. Perhaps the difference between Wade and his predecessors in these deserts was the complete dedication of Wade, to the point where he was willing to lay down his life for the cause he had espoused, whereas the explorers had neither wish nor intention to die in that wilderness.

Wade's report to the Surveyor-General was made on his personal inspection of that vast area already described.

Perhaps no immediate decision was possible for Wade's suggestions to be made legal in the allocating of this, a third of the land mass of Australia, as an Aboriginal reserve. The actual Land Act defining the reserves was delayed for a number of years. The actual boundaries we had defined were the north end of the Nullarbor extending from Mount Eva to Kalgoorlie as a southern boundary, and from Mount Eva to one hundred miles west of Tennant Creek as an eastern border. From Tennant Creek to the eastern edge of settlement in Western Australia as a northern line, and a line joining the western extremity of the south and north lines as a western boundary.

We knew this would be too drastic for the powers-that-be in the Lands Departments of the three States involved but, when the boundaries were finally drawn, it should be noted that the areas we defined are still at this time, seventy years later, as undeveloped as they were in our travels. The boundaries have been enlarged on the eastern side by giving the Everard Ranges and land as far as 'Granite Downs' to the Aborigines. Parts of the Kimberley are now included in the gazetted Aboriginal lands, but no attempt has been made to extend the lands leased to white settlers into the desert regions.

If I might make a suggestion for the future of the lands described here, and for the most part gazetted as Aboriginal lands, it's this:

The basic need of all people, all land and all development is water. A major water conservation program in the various deserts over the area of Wade's travels would make possible settlements that could accommodate the rapidly expanding population of the tribes today.

Only one stumbling block need be overcome to achieve successful development here and that would be the absolute prohibition of liquor, which could, and does, ruin the Aboriginal people everywhere it is available.

As of now, the 'Ernabella' settlement, which is large and prospering, has a total ban on liquor.

There is absolutely no doubt that Solomon's maxim:

Righteousness exaltath a nation

sounds puritanical. But it is true.

When Giles, Forrest, Carnegie, Gregory, Warburton, Leichhardt and others who left no writings, had looked at the deserts Wade chose as his parish, they were inspired to explore — and sometimes they perished — in an effort to open inland Australia to settlement. Or, as in the case of Giles, they sought a possible cattle route from the eastern settlements to a West Australian market. This is a typical summation of their findings.

From Ernest Giles' diary, October 1874:

Although I have here and there found places where scanty supplies of the element of water were to be found, yet they are at such enormous distances apart and the regions in which they exist are of so utterly worthless a kind that it seems to be intended by the great creator that civilised beings should never re-enter here.

Giles reported to his sponsor, Sir Thomas Elder, that the country he had twice travelled was unsuitable for overlanding cattle.

It is impossible in a story of this kind, where the principal theme is the life and work of Bill Wade, to do more than tell his story. Nevertheless the deserts he adopted, which were the home of his Aboriginal people, need description because their harshness enhances the courage of one who, knowing well the field of his endeavours, still felt the call to not only make the inhabitants his people, but also to make their vast inhospitable land his home.

The years 1873–74 saw considerable exploration activity in the desert areas by men of scientific bent. Giles did

excellent work in the botanical field. Warburton and Carnegie kept meticulous diaries of each day's travel and included a description of trees and landscape. Their weakness, if it can be called such, was their attitude and handling of the Aborigines which was so different from that of Wade who, as a late arrival, inherited a widespread attitude of hostility. This I have been at some care to record, along with the way Wade was able to quickly gather the Aborigines into his welcoming arms. He loved them, cared for them, and spent the rest of his life in great endeavour for them.

I believe that he did not give his life in vain.

Crossing the Desert Without Water

In 1927, we were making east again to the station country and supplies. We were now out of water. The day was blisteringly hot. It would be our last day if we didn't find water soon. South from the Musgraves, Wade had looked to faraway mountains, deciding as usual that these also were his parish. We had spent five days plodding down the dry bed of the creek that runs from Mount Woodroffe to the Everard Ranges expecting — hoping — to find water somewhere at the foot of the range before us.

The dog pads were days old, the waters dried back to soup. One deep rock hole was full of decaying bodies, not even sieving or boiling could bring water out of that putrid soup. Perishing camels would not look at it. There was no return, not in that heat. Wade had come forward to the lead as we plodded eastward between the ranges, looking for tracks that might lead to water.

A track, a deep, dusty pad made by kangaroos, for there were no cattle as far west as those ranges, went north and south. The choice was ours. One way could lead to water. The plain was wide. We turned north. That Bill Wade believed in miracles, I am sure. But whether he did on this desperate day I cannot say, as his face was set, rigid, unreadable. Low hills showed across the plain to the north — bare sunburned rock and granite monoliths. We were a weary caravan, slowly approaching the sheer face of the rock rising out of the plain. I hooshed the camels down, tying their front legs, for the camels were restless and thirsty. They would take any opportunity to leave us on a desperate return to the water we had left days ago.

Wade climbed away to the east, I took the steeper face to the north of west, clambering slowly to the heights above, looking for cracks in the rock but doubtful, for it had been months since any rain had fallen. Sometimes water will lie deep in the granite cracks for months, sheltered by the overhang from the sun. I climbed higher, higher, until at last, about noontime, I looked over the top to the ranges far away to the north. It was quiet, not a breath of air. The sun beat down. I was thirsty, fearful this could be the end of the road. I was without Wade's faith.

I sat, searching the rocky face of the bald mountain with careful appraisal for what could be a rock hole with water. Eye distance away to the right, a crack in the great rocky dome looked interesting. And it was. As I climbed barefoot across the dome, a pigeon rose from the crack. There were bees there, deep in the crack, where they drank from what looked like wet mud. It was too far down

and too narrow for me to get there, but the rock seemed deeply riven. It could even be split right to ground level.

I climbed, sliding down the rock face to investigate. At the foot of the mountain, there was a cave-like entrance beneath the rock face. Low, almost too low, but a big-enough-sized hole for me to crawl on my belly, following the tunnel-like crack. Several yards in, the skeleton of a wallaby almost stopped my progress. But then I felt that the sandy bottom was damp. A few more feet and the sand was wet. I scooped it with my hands.

Here was water. Backing slowly, almost painfully, I was glad indeed to feel the light coming from the entrance. There, waiting, was Wade. He had found nothing. Without a word, he looked at the mud on my fingers. His first words were typical of his lately made Salvation Army friends: 'Praise the Lord.' I agreed. Taking two buckets, I crawled deep into the burrow-like tunnel, altogether bringing seventeen hard-won buckets out.

'Saved' again: Once more this man, whose faith had taken a blind leap into unknown lands, had won.

If by chance some adventurous young person should like to look for and find this tunnel which saved our lives, it is almost north of Monolith Ilbilla in the Everard Ranges, which is now an Aboriginal reserve. The approach from the south is flat, the range bearing the cave lies east–west. The distance from the main range is about ten miles. The direction from the blue soak at 'Moorilyanna' is west of south-west, about a day or two walk to the mount. This would, by estimate, be due west several days travel on foot from 'Granite Downs', which is now a roadside stop on the new road from the south to Alice Springs.

No such roads existed in 1927. There have been great changes in that country in the past seventy years. The Everard Ranges are now Aboriginal reserve. The country was taken up as a cattle station years after Wade's time and called 'Everard Park'. It was later abandoned and given to the Aborigines as part of the huge reserve.

A Day With Wade

In 1928, we were travelling past the Mann Ranges — about the border area — and had as yet made no contact with the tribes of that place. Although the day was early, the sun not yet showing over the eastern ranges, we had packed up and were on our way. The big proud gelding, called a bullock in camel language, was leading the string. We were headed north, trying to find a way out of the maze of granite cliff hills that surround Mount Mann on the Northern Territory border. Wade was walking at the back of the last camel in the string, watching out for any load which might be slipping. I was walking, with the lead nose line in my hand, picking the way forwards among the rocks.

The night had been calm, one of those nights when no breath of air disturbs the absolute peace of a desert night. But I had spent a restless night because in the evening I had disturbed a small family of Aborigines as I walked up a gorge looking for water. In my hand there had been a can kept for just this sort of search for water in the rocky hills.

I had almost walked into their camp. They had been sitting by their fire and my bare feet made little noise on the dusty ground. The man picked up his spears as he half turned with a yell, almost a shout. His woman and children ran screaming into the rocky hillside. These were people who had not seen a white man nor a shiny object like my can. They were of a small tribe living north of the Mann Ranges, people of the Gibson Desert. Although this was 1928, these people had as yet made no European contact. Those who had heard of white intruders were not favourably impressed with tales of the 'shoot on sight' attitude of some the explorers, or the taking of captives (see Giles' diary) as guides. The presence of a timid tribe was enough to send me scurrying back to the camp, which was not more than a mile away. I knew by the threatening cries that 'discretion was the better part . . . '

Without too much argument, Wade and I saddled up and headed out to the sandhills. It was late in the day, which I knew would be too near dark for any attack by the tribe, which would have been alerted to the 'enemy' in the area.

As I have written, the night was calm — not a sound. Likely as not we had been scouted, for the night noises were silenced, which meant someone was out there, looking us over. Next day we were early away as the camels had been knee-hobbled. It was usual to hobble short or tie down the camels when they might wander away to feed overnight, sometimes quite far from the camp.

At daybreak I heard a chant far away to the south but did not reckon on any appearance of warriors. But they came, banded together, from a rocky outcrop to the near south. It was too late for me to hoosh the nearest lead camel down.

Wade stood with arms outstretched shouting welcome to a frenzied chanting bank of spearmen. I watched in wonder as Wade put his arms about the painted leader, speaking the only word for 'welcome friend' he knew — 'yemeragee, yemeragee'.

The next move had to be mine, but I stood dumb and wondering. The tribe gathered around, fingering the ropes, pulling the long hair on the camels. There had to be trouble. One camel only had to kick or bite to start some eager young spearman wanting one of our large beasts for a feast. We had to go. No doubt Wade would have stopped and camped there and then, but the mood of the warriors was not settled in my opinion, and I persuaded Wade to travel on.

North past the Petermann Ranges and across another almost waterless stretch, we went on with our mission of inspection to cover that million square miles of the almost unknown. We made forty miles that day. My excuse for travelling so far was that we did not know where we would find the next water. But that was only part of the reason. I also wanted to put as much distance as possible between us and the possibly hostile tribe. If Bill Wade had a weakness, it was his insatiable hunger to see new people. It was also a hunger to see new country. He was the perfect explorer, going where water was unknown, meeting people who were obviously and nervously hostile.

The Petermann Ranges was the place where Lasseter would leave his bones. Stories, which drifted back to me years later, indicated that Lasseter might have had reasons for staying with the Petermann Ranges tribe for, at the time of his historic death, Wade and I were within message distance of the tribe, who said nothing of his presence to us. He could also have walked back to the eastern stations. Old tribesmen have told me their opinion of Lasseter, who had little knowledge of their tribal customs.

The Aborigines could send messages from one place to faraway places by signals between families and tribes. My own experience has provided evidence that these communications were possible.

When a man called Davis went into the Musgraves from Oodnadatta in 1927, the tribes in the Mann Ranges knew of his unwelcome behaviour. They were able to tell me this as, by then, I had an increasing knowledge of their language. This message had travelled across three hundred miles in a land where there were no roads, or telephones, or European settlement. The messages could have been passed by complicated smoke signals or by telepathy. As there is doubt in my mind of the restricted detail that it is possible to send by smoke signal, then I believe there has to be some transmission by telepathy.

Chapter 9

Tribal Justice

*By the following
night, after our
companion had fled,
we knew that our
successful return could
be a near thing.*

The Desert

Wade paid scant heed to the dangers of the unknown. He was serving a caring Master, in whose hands he was placed.

Winter was about over. There had been rainwater in the rock holes and soaks were plentiful. Heading west from the West Australian border ranges, a friendly tribe caught up with us about mid-morning. The men and youths were combing a low range of hills to the north for game.

Our usual way was along the easy going, on the valleys or plains. With us, chattering along, were children and young women, all collecting grubs, rabbits or whatever could be gathered without losing sight of our interesting cavalcade of camels. A pair of girls trotted along beside Bill Wade trying to talk but, of course, Bill could only smile and chatter away in his own Cockney lingo. One healthy-looking teenage girl kept offering Wade a rabbit just caught. He, being high up on his camel, leaned down to either reject or accept the offering. He must have leaned over too far when the camel surged and unseated him. He was caught in one stirrup and dragged. The camel kicked out, landing him fair on the side of the face. I feared for him because it was a nasty blow. He was dragged a few steps until the stirrup broke and he fell. There was not a word from Bill that night. He was obviously badly hurt. (He probably put the punishment down to looking too hard at the unclad females.)

Leaving that happy, friendly family of tribesmen and women with regret, we turned north across the track taken by others in the past century without finding any evidence that others had passed this way. We were now close by where Gibson died but we found no traces of him, nor did the tribes seem to remember Gibson or Giles, his leader. Of course, it had been long before.

Other explorers, such as Forrest, had crossed the desert lower down. Most of the trips made by Forrest had been across the area above the Nullarbor Plain and south of the Deering Hills, missing the Warburton Range to their north.

We were now north of Latitude Hill, far north of Mount Mann past the Petermann Ranges. How we knew roughly where we were was by sighting the highest mountains. Although these high mountain pinnacles were too far apart to see even with good glasses, we knew within a hundred miles or so where they should be. But we were now in country where no explorers had left marked places, if they had ever been there, which was doubtful. We saw no signs, nor heard of them from the Pitjantjara tribesmen. Although my ability to speak to the tribes in their language was limited, I was able to converse a little, but not enough to ask about their contact with explorers.

We were far out in the direction of Sturt Creek and the Tanami Desert towards Halls Creek but without means of knowing just where. A native lad, almost a warrior, had joined up with us north of the Petermanns. It was evident that this was his country for he knew all the little rock holes, the native wells. At times it occurred to me that these were too small for return waters as our camels took a big toll of the meagre supply, leaving little or nothing for a return journey. Nevertheless, when we found creeks running from north to south, we knew that in an emergency we could continue north to the fringes of the Kimberley waters.

Full of fun this native lad was. I enjoyed his company as he laughed at my attempts to say the words which rolled off his tongue. Enough of what he said let me know that he was making for big water. I believed him, although at every water on the way, the canteens were topped up. Came the day when his face took on a sober look. Somehow he sensed that the water in the promised land had dried up. It could have been the absence of fresh tracks — no dog pads, no water birds.

The night before we reached the area where the big water was to be, we camped in a shallow creek flat, a dry camp. Our guide, the happy youth, drank an extraordinary amount of water from the canteen. As usual he made a little fire close by, ate his share of the meal and, like us, lay down on the ground to sleep. In the morning he was gone. Perhaps I should have set about to track him back to known waters. But with the exuberance of youth, plus Wade's now long history of survival, we carried on to the north. By midday, we were traversing a low series of white quartz hills which cut the camels' feet badly, leaving a smear of blood as they went. By the following night, after our companion had fled, we knew that our successful return could be a near thing.

The country was mainly spinifex and sand with small rocky outcrops. We retraced our track, using the low-lying areas of soft sand between the quartz to save the camels' feet. Back to 'desertion' camp. It seemed logical that our young man guide, the deserter, would head like a homing pigeon for known water or his people — which is what he did.

Tracks stay visible for a long time in those crusty desert sands. His incredible flight, without stopping for rest, was evident as we tracked him back. His tracks showed no place where he had rested or watered. We were making twenty-five to thirty miles a day, barely stopping to rest. When we did, we tied the

camels down with knee to neck hobbles, for there was no water nor little feed for them. We had learned by experience that thirsty camels, if they are allowed to graze, will set out in single file travelling direct to some known water. This has happened to people who, from bitter experience, learned not to let thirsty camels graze, even in hobbles.

Next time I saw the absconded lad he met me like a long-lost brother. No doubt he had thought we would perish.

Having retreated from the northern desert, called the Tanami, where we had had hopes of finding the big water, it occurred to me that what might have scared our guide boy was that he had passed beyond his tribal boundary, or that the tribes had placed a taboo on the disclosure of their precious water. This was quite likely as we experienced their reluctance to show hidden waters. Often the entrance to rock holes were covered, probably to hide them or to keep game from fouling them. Native wells we invariably had to clean to get the soakage working. The water was always slightly foul in those leafy rotting sand soaks.

Nothing daunted our retreat and close shave with the perilous final dash for water when the northern penetration failed. Wade decided to attack the Gibson Desert west of the Petermann Ranges looking for another of the big waters which the friendly Pitjantjara people had hinted were there (a long way west). They had offered no help to guide the way.

Leaving friendly tribes was always a hard parting, for although Wade did not, or could not, learn their words, he loved to teach the children his gospel songs. Sixty years later I found an old man who had been a child at the Gibson Desert camp and who remembered the old songs. It is now over seventy years since I listened to Wade sing his gospel songs to the naked children about his camp fire, sometimes with their interested parents standing back in the shadows:

Deep, deep is the ocean
Wide as the wide blue sea

This was Bill Wade's version; even the tune sticks in my mind and, given a wide space and no audience, I sing it to myself. Then there was some 'Halabulah' song which the kids loved, but I have forgotten. The old people at 'Ernabella' in the Musgraves still remember Wade as the 'Halabulah' man. If Wade were one of the Pope's men, he would have been sainted long ago and I, as his 'devil's advocate', would have to approve.

Paddy and Victor

Losing camels in that desert is a sure way to death, as Lasseter found several years later. And again, in 1929, Paddy DeConlay, with Victor Dumas, had let their camels go in hobbles south of Ayers Rock. They were exploring, having come from the Oodnadatta district. Victor set out in the morning to get their camels, which had been hobbled out to graze overnight, leaving Paddy on a dry camp. Victor was away for weeks. Paddy told me the story of how, when Victor did not return, he had carried his pack bags, one by one, twenty miles to a water. He had left a note on a tree in case Victor came back, which Victor did. Victor had tracked the camels right across the desert from a place south-west of what is now known as Ayers Rock, living off the land, finding water in rock holes and native wells and eventually catching the camels near the settled country, which is the north–south line to Alice Springs. It was an incredible feat of bushcraft. Victor Dumas was an extraordinary bushman, as was his companion Paddy DeConlay.

Perhaps I might diverge here to put on record a few episodes in Paddy's life as they occurred during my association with him, both then and later. In some ways, Paddy's and Bill Wade's lives ran parallel. In one week I saw some offended would-be husband try to shoot the offending Paddy, and some unknown try to kill him with a knife. One would have to be quick to be successful in any attempt to kill Patrick. He was smart, one who might be called a typical stockman — bow-legged and spritely in his movements. If he had a conscience, it never showed, for conscience was an extravagance he could not afford.

When the government of the day, in 1928, passed a decree that all white men living with Aboriginal women would be required to either marry them legally or get rid of

them as sleeping partners, Paddy solved the problem by marrying a white bar girl he picked up (I was his best man). Meanwhile, he kept the harem close by and a serious attempt was organised by the Aboriginal husbands of the borrowed wives to liquidate the offender. But Paddy got in first and managed to liquidate the conspirators. Duly charged with a capital crime, Paddy claimed self-defence, which the judge accepted.

Just a few grogs and the Irish background of the DeConlays would come to life with a fine camp fire concert of Irish songs, always ending with the singer passing out there by the fire and sleeping the sleep of the unfettered. A fine horseman, Paddy would often camp alone for weeks on a far-out lonely waterhole, track-riding the cattle, riding the desert tablelands of the Abminga area, a country where men disappear and are never found. Paddy was the kind of man who would risk his life, but I doubt if he was ever lost.

Strange as it might seem to the rest of the world, who have always slept in comfortable beds or never faced the bullet or the knife in anger, Paddy did had a few loyal friends. His luck produced a draw for a block of land in the western fringe of the cattle lands. He called it 'Mount Conners'. Old Jim Mortimer, a cattle man (once my partner in an early enterprise), offered to help Paddy stock the place with cattle. There Paddy battled the droughts, lived with the things he loved, and died, buried where he would want to be.

Food of the Desert

In the 1920s, few men lived in that vast hinterland of Australia. Most of those who did knew, or were known to, all the others who made this wilderness their home. Wade always rated as a stranger in that western land. He saw all those he met as prospective candidates for conversion. Often when he tackled men like the camel man, Gool Mahommet, or other sunburned case-hardened sinners who never knew what his speech was all about, I wondered at his desperate strategy of propagating his faith. But who knows if there is any other way? Paul did it. Luther and Saint Peter were men preaching their faith with dramatic, long-term effect. Some became martyrs. Others laid down their lives in long-term loneliness, as did Bill Wade.

Most of the Gibson, Victoria, and the Simpson deserts which I now know well, are not all flat featureless plains like the country around Maree or Oodnadatta. The country is often rolling sand dunes or rocky creeks and small gibber plains in the case of the country between the central Australian ranges, such as the Musgraves and Mann group.

In the far south, vast scrub of mallee-type eucalyptus grows dense and low, quite featureless except for occasional hillocks where on stony cliffs the wild fig grows. These figs have a special attraction to the vegetable-starved Aborigines who travel long distances to eat the fig in season. At the same time as the fig gets yellow ripe, so do small fruit called quandongs which grow in isolated patches over the southern desert. The fruit is red-ripe, making the trees look more ornamental when the peach-like fruit ripens. The seed is large with a fruit that is good to eat even though the flesh is thin and slightly tart.

The women of the desert people dry the skin of the quandong and pack it into cakes. The dried cakes last for years, as evident when the Willorara stored them in the Nullarbor caves as provident rations for when they and their women were raided.

It was a time of figs and quandongs when Wade elected to go south to meet the families migrating down into this sparse land:

We paid the price and went.

Water in the mallee desert is scarce. What there is occurs in shallow wells or a little after rain in rock holes. There were a few shallow lakes further west. I had heard stories of a mysterious big water (Caabi Buulka) further south. But no tribesman or woman would offer to lead us to it. Not till later did the story of that deep water come to me, although neither Wade nor I ever saw it. We were told the water was deep in the earth and had to be approached through a narrow limestone cave. This was a place of refuge for the Willorara tribe — for when the fierce woman-hunting warriors of the Musgraves raided the small group living north of the great Nullarbor Plain.

Second-hand although the story was, it was told me by Akbar Khan who, by now, had married Lali, the Willorara girl. He told us of the deep cave that contained water at a low level, far down, reached only by steps cut into dangerous slopes. This cave was a refuge prepared with wood and winnowed grain, dried figs and quandongs, which were stored for the occasions when women fled there for safety. Mysterious noises produced through hollow wooden pipes kept the illusion of mystery from attack by other tribes. (It is now known that the Nullarbor contains deep caves such as the one Akbar told me about.)

There is a series of limestone caves with water west of the South Australian–Northern Territory border about a hundred miles inside Western Australia. This cavern had a small entrance and led to a series of water excavated caves. This water I would guarantee to be permanent.

Such water, if developed, could be the basis of a settlement. It must be exploited for otherwise how will all

the people who are multiplying now and being fed rations supplied by the Commonwealth survive when the national aid ceases for some catastrophic reason or economic drought. Water and effort could make the desert blossom.

The Law-breakers

We were on our way again. We had spelled our camels well, where good water was available, we'd mended the packs;and double-bagged the sugar, flour and other cereals carried in bags as either top loading or in boxes. The thick mallee had worn the corners of the loading. The animals' backs were in good order, all with hard humps showing that they were picking up. We were ready now for the desert again. I have looked up an old diary written in 1927, the pages very faded, almost gone in places, the writing was in pencil and some pages were water stained. One date, still legible, is September 30, 1927. It says, 'spent the day patching the spear wounds'.

The night had been noisy, filled with shouts, screams, occasionally a piteous sob, like a death rattle. Wade and I were camped under the overhang of a granite cliff, where echoes of the enactment on the sweeping plain ahead, reverberated. The night was dead calm with stars clear as only the desert stars can be. An all-day corroboree had ended in a judgement session.

This was a gathering of many tribes, including some individuals I had met two deserts away. What wrongs had to be avenged I did not know. But at least one young fellow, who came with a spear through the thick of his neck, which had evidently missed the artery or windpipe and spine, must have overstepped a basic rule because legs are usually the target. Or death. We cut off the tapered end of the spear where there are two joins. The sharp, hard end of the spear is usually the heart wood of the tchilga bush. Then comes the expendable thin wood about two feet long attached to the body of the spear by wallaby sinew.

He was very stoical as we washed his wounds and poured disinfectant onto the holes. We did not bind up his neck as he wanted to cover the holes with the ash of the tchilga bush (one of the wattle family). We knew the ash of this bush is a powerful healer, as we had previously witnessed its power. I never saw this young man again, but he could be alive today as he was about my own age at the time. We did not stay with this tribe which had been mostly friendly.

The next victim had five holes through his upper leg, where he had pulled spears out. Wade gave him a shirt, dressed the wounds, and then went back to the battle-wounded. No women were hurt or, if they were, probably death would have been the verdict.

One old man who was likely the keeper of tribal lore, a sort of witchdoctor who made rain, was the one who decided who should die. He was a tribal chief who also posed as healer by magic. He and several others were walking alongside and around and behind me as I carried the camel nose lines on my way to track down the camels. Although the bells had been quite plain a few hours before, the animals could not have gotten far in hobbles. A strange look came on a lad by my side which alerted me to turn quickly. The old chief had his waddy fighting stick raised in the act of striking me on the head. Caught in the act, he lowered the stick onto my shoulder. It was almost an apology. I thought then and still do that the untutored wild tribes of the west were children at heart, some good, some bad but never the devious villains of our

own sophisticated civilisation. They all laughed it off. But I took a precaution of shooting a kangaroo for them to show what magic my walking stick could do. They had never seen a gun before. They named it 'poweranditchic' a word hard to say but having coined it there and then it showed initiative. I used the word a lot after that.

I later broke the stock off my old gun and could not use it, but by this time I was ready to hunt without it. Nevertheless a man unarmed has a lot of trusting to do.

Including women, children, old men and old women and young warriors, the assembly at the big council at the south Musgraves added up to more than a thousand. This was the largest assembly we encountered. The next largest gathering, where spears were hurled, was far to the west on the edge of the Great Victoria Desert. There no casualties were seen. We hear talk of Aboriginal law and culture from the late day descendants of the tribal people but they have no longer tribal ancient medicine men, no gaols of their own, nor kadaicha men to carry out the death punishments.

A new system of law enforcement would have to be developed if the descendants of our dark people were to set up another nation. There is no question now that these, our indigenous people, must become one with us and accept the laws acceptable to all nations' codes, which are devised to restrict anarchy. And, as I have said before, they must develop living habits as herdsmen or horticulture farmers of some kind. They need to establish new totems, new marriage laws, new penal codes. This judgement is for the tribes now long since dispersed. Only the desert peoples are still able to remember their codes and these groups are fast losing their old wise men or respect for those they have.

Chapter 10

Gold in the Hills

*Bill Wade and
I were young in
1926—28, he with
the fire of a
new-found faith and
me with the fire of
youth and adventure.*

The Lost Goldmine

My old diary does not tell me of the immediate days after heading west from the shelter of the Petermann Ranges on the West Australian Gibson Desert side. But from memory, in the days immediately after leaving the shelter and safety of the Petermanns, we followed rock holes, which was risky for any return journey because they dry out quickly. We were looking for a more permanent supply on which to make a depot from where we could explore a hundred miles in each direction. The place we found has no known name, nor is it listed as being on any explorers' route. There were no Pitjantjara families camped there. The area was limestone with some deep pit-like holes on its rocky surface. One such hole led into a cave-like limestone room in which lay a pool of what looked like permanent water. This was another milestone camp for us in locating areas. It was a place to come back to if we explored south, north and west. North of this camp I call 'the cave', we came across another quartz-like hill. The quartz was white with dark streaks, perhaps an experienced prospector would have considered it a prospect. This was 1927.

Years later I was shown a bag of similar quartz rock streaked with visible gold. The man who showed it to me was called Jim Prince. He was the wifley table worker — the wifley table being a table built on a slanting principle so it tilts two ways and rocks — on a mine I was running with Al McDonald. We were mining for wolfram and the place was called Mosquito Creek. In a secretive sort of way the old fellow, who had one gammy foot, took me into his tent and poured out the quartz samples on his bed. I was excited to see the samples so evidently rich in gold.

'Where did you get this?' I asked.

Prince said, 'I was out west of the Petermanns and short of tucker. I could not stay long but I'd like to go back.'

'Would you take me?' I asked. I told him that I had some camels not far away at a place called Frew River. These were camels I'd had brought up from Maree by two girls who were looking for an adventure (both of these girls are still alive).

Prince hesitated. 'No more camels for me,' he said. 'With my lame foot I would never get back if I lost the camels. I would be like that stupid Lasseter who lost his life looking for gold he never found.'

I said, 'Yes! I know about Lasseter. He came out to the Petermanns after Wade and I had been there a year or so. It is evident that he couldn't find gold or he would have had samples with him when he died. He lost his camels because he was no camel man, or he would have done what Victor Dumas did in the Musgraves when his camels cleared out. He walked after them and brought them back.'

'Will you stake me to a plane?' Prince asked. I agreed, thinking of the quartz hills Wade and I had seen years earlier in that area. I went immediately south to arrange for an adventurous pilot with a plane. While I was away looking for the plane, Kurt Johannsen of Alice Springs met Prince and offered to take him out in his plane. I knew Prince had been where he said he had because he knew the place as well as I did. When I quizzed him on his knowledge of the desert west of the Petermanns, he gave the right answers.

Jim Prince and Kurt Johannsen took off in the light single-engine plane on their historic flight. Before they left, my enterprising brother-in-law, H. V. Leonard, signed Prince up on a contract which Prince later discarded.

Here is reference to it dated 20th December, 1950:

43–48 Albion House,
Waymouth Street,
Adelaide,
20th December, 1950
A. H. Telfer Esq.,
Under Secretary for Mines
Mines Department
PERTH W.A.

Dear Mr. Telfer,

When in Perth recently I spoke to you about a matter concerning a client of mine. One James A. Prince, a prospector, approached me to finance a trip to the area in W.A. between the Kintore and Rawlinson Ranges near the W.A. – N.T. border west and south-west of Alice Springs. His statement was that he had previously been over a large auriferous area there, and he produced a quantity of specimen stone alleged to have then been secured by him.

The parties reached agreement, and following instructions received, I prepared an Agreement providing inter alia for my client to finance an expedition, to be guided by Prince, for the purpose of locating the area, and subsequently pegging and applying for reserves and leases there over in the name of my client or his nominees. This Agreement was executed by the parties, and a sum sufficient to cover the cost of the expedition was paid into my trust account with instruction as to its disbursement. It was a term of the Agreement that Prince should make his knowledge available to my client only.

After some differences regarding the personnel of the expedition, a matter which under the Agreement was within the sole decision of my client, Prince evidently decided to ignore the Agreement, as he was next heard of through press reports as having set out with a companion,

Kurt Johannsen, of Alice Springs. Their trip ended with their plane being disabled and Johannsen flying back with a damaged propeller, leaving Prince in the desert, where he was subsequently picked up. Johannsen has since acknowledged having read the Agreement. It is not considered likely that Prince located the reef, but I have been instructed to ask that, if either of the men named should apply for the grant of any form of mining tenement in the area named, information of any such application be notified to me, and Search Certificates supplied, so that any action necessary to protect my client's rights may be taken. You were good enough to say that you will, on receipt of a letter from me setting out the above facts, circularise your Department with instructions to the above effect.

Wishing you the compliments of the Season

Yours faithfully

H. V. LEONARD

Dare-devil Flight Out of a Desert

Kurt's most famous journey was out in the dry lands. In 1950, he and two mates headed off to the west from Alice Springs to investigate the old Lasseter's reef of gold claims.

They set off with two trucks and a light plane and after making a base camp at Mount Lyell, Brown, Kurt and Jim Prince — the prospector — made a reconnaissance flight.

Kurt was the pilot, having learned to fly at Parafield airport near Adelaide. They had taken spare fuel with them and refuelled as planned when they found a flat salt lake called Lake Hopkins. Everything went well, except that as they taxied to take off again, one wheel sank suddenly down through the crust of the lake into the sludge beneath. The plane nosedived forward and the beautifully symmetrical propeller ploughed into the surface, splintering off its ends.

But, unlike Burke and Wills, or Lasseter himself, Kurt and Jimmy had some bushcraft. Kurt rigged up a little water condenser, using two petrol cans, to get pure water from the salty brine beneath the lake's surface. He'd used the broken-off bits of the propeller to dig a little well down to the water level. Then they sat and waited, but Kurt tired of this. He decided to try evening up the propeller blade, using a hacksaw blade and an axe. When he was satisfied, he summoned up his courage and decided to fly the plane.

Modern-day pilots will not fly with even a tiny chip in the propeller, but Kurt was preparing to take off with about half the usual width of the propeller. Jimmy was left behind to wait, at the salt lake.

'I thought I wasn't going to make it,' said Kurt later. 'The plane wouldn't go up above about 200 feet. It was just sort of hanging there, and the revs were way up past the limit.'

But then he spotted an eagle, just hanging there too, but much higher up. There was a life-saving thermal and Kurt got himself and his plane into it. There were more eagles and more thermals, and eventually Kurt made it back to the base camp.

Meanwhile the alarm had been raised that the two men were missing in the 'waterless Central Australian desert'. An RAAF bomber had been sent down from Darwin to search for them. It actually flew over the camp and did not see the men's signals for help.

Kurt then drove back into town in the remaining truck and made arrange-ments to fly out and pick up Jimmy Prince, who returned safe and sound, having lived off native plants.

The propeller now has a pride of place in Kurt's house, a delightful light-filled home he has built himself on a piece of land on the outskirts of Alice Springs.

The Mysterious Jim Prince

When Jim Prince returned after his close shave with death, he disappeared. Years later I received this letter:

Dear Mr. Williams,

I was browsing through a book shop the other day and I came across a book by you dealing with men that you had met or worked with in your earlier years. Unfortunately, the name escapes me at present. One of the men featured in the book was a Jim Prince whom you had worked with in the Northern Territory. I believe that I know this man and I thought that you might be interested in the little bit of information that I can give you about him.

From 1952 to 1955 I worked as a Jackaroo on Waterloo Station in the East Kimberley's in the Northern

Territory. This property was one of the Vestey holdings in the N.T. and my father (Bob McLachlan) was the manager. During this time we had the usual turn-over in station Cooks, it being fairly hard to find a good one and when we did they tended to get itchy-feet after a while and take-off for Wyndham or Halls Creek. My Dad always said that their skin was cracking for a good booze-up. Anyway, at some stage in those years, Dad was sent a cook who was the aforementioned Jim Prince and he stayed quite a fair time as far as cooks go. Now Jim was a small man, probably 50 to 60 years old, with a full head of greying hair, and a very pronounced limp. I gathered that he had injured his hip in earlier years and the leg was a little shorter than the other. Jim was a quiet man, kept to himself, spoke in short, terse sentences, and I never knew him to smile. I was of the impression that he had known a lot of pain in his time. He was a very courteous man and a reasonable cook. My mother always told a story about Jim concerning, I think, rock cakes. I can't be absolutely sure about the type of cakes but I do believe that they were rock cakes. Anyway, Mum asked Jim if he knew how to cook cakes and he replied 'Yes' and suggested rock cakes. Mum said that would be fine and could he make some for smoko. Well, from that moment on all we ever got from Jim at smoko time was rock cakes, until Mum had to finally tell him that the rock cakes were fine but, did he know how to make scones? I gather that we had scones from then on.

You will see from the following report, which is a copy of a government paper — an attempt to follow the Jim Prince story — that Jim never told the truth. Only one who had been in the actual area where Jim found his samples could have verified his story, which is what I did. Either Bill Wade or I would have been able to check on Prince's story.

He gave them a location several hundred miles to the south of where he and Johannsen wrecked the plane.

Anyone who has tried to locate a place from the air would know what an impossible task Jim had set both himself and Kurt Johannsen. I do not know the salt lake they crashed on but do know that it was not even close to the quartz hills that Jim described to me.

Many have tried to get me to take them to the location but at my age and with the success of my own goldmine behind me, I do not need to walk, fly or go by camel to that dreary area. It is a task for a young man.

As I have written, Bill Wade and I were young in 1926–28, he with the fire of a new-found faith and me with the fire of youth and adventure. Sometimes I wonder why I did not write to Wade in his camp at the lonely Rawlinson and tell him of the interest in the quartz hills, but I doubt if he would have cared.

The last word on Prince's search for gold is a description of his journey contained in the following letter from the Commissioner of Native Welfare.

District Officer,
Central,
Perth.
Subject :   Food and Water Supplies — Central Reserve
Reference   :   CD 24–1/2 dated 22.8.58

The Director of Welfare, Darwin advises as follows :—

Further to your letter of 27th August, 1958, please find enclosed the only known information on Prince's trips.

We then went on to Lyell Brown Hills and west from there from rockhole to rockhole till we struck the ironstone country fourteen miles south of the Kintore Range. We turned south then and went round the southern end of Lake McDonald, passed on the north side of the Bonython Range in Western Australia, kept on the south side of the Turner Hills and went west about thirty miles. We got a road through the sandhills and travelled south about thirty miles to a place called Chilla — this means permanent water in the native dialect. We then went on the camels to the Rawlinson Range to the supposed Lasseter Reef. From there we came back on our tracks to Alice Springs where I went immediately to Dr. Lum at the hospital as I had been poisoned by the water at Turner Hills. At that place I drank water from a rockhole and had every symptom of being poisoned. The native in that country poison one hole with a plant that is known as Emu poison. The holes they do not poison they cover over but the poisoned one they leave uncovered. This seems to be a prevalent practice in that country as there is almost no game there now. The bush used for the poisoning is one that grows on the sandhills with a corky white bark which higher up becomes smooth. It has a long narrow green leaf. It is deadly poison and camels die very quickly if they eat any of it. The natives grind up the dried leaves into powder and then put the powder into water.'

No Officers of this Branch have located this particular soakage to date and it is therefore impossible to give any accurate information as to whether or not it is permanent.

Commissioner of Native Welfare.

A pioneer traveller called Lindsay had made a brief trip through the Everards in the 1870s, noting that there was a large rock hole in those ranges. Bill Wade and I had found this hole filled with putrid dead bodies of kangaroos and wallabies which had fallen into its steep depth. This shows how one could not rely on any reports of rock holes or native wells.

We found that over a period of dry months there were very few reliable waters in the area of range and desert. Perhaps in those days the small supply of water in the shallow native wells would suffice for a family. But with camels, which can drink twenty gallons at a time when they are dry, a water has to be larger than the usual rock hole to give a team of camels a drink. I was sympathetic to tribal families who existed on small waters when camels came by and drank it all.

David Carnegie in 1896 reported a good water in an area about one hundred and fifty miles west of Lake McKay, but this we never found, although it could have been only a mile or so off — one has only to experience the vastness of this desert to see how necessary it would be to have a tribesman as guide. This is not always possible because of tribal boundaries.

To those who go out looking for Lasseter's Reef, or Prince's gold, I say that the salt lake that Jim Prince and Kurt Johannsen landed on could have been any one of many. Jim had told of his find being north of the Warburtons, which would have been Lake McDonald. But from first-hand talk of water holes and notable points, I believe Jim's gold is south of Lake McKay, west of the West Australian border marked by Latitude Hill.

Dewey PS 33 : 13 - 15

Chapter 11

Thieves
and
Missions

Glancing at the wooden
dishes ... I saw my
aluminium drinking
vessel, stolen from
that camp in the gorge.

Drama at Wade's Camp

Wade had set up cam, at the western end of the Mann Ranges in a rocky gorge with water far up where the climb was for bare feet on slippery rocks. The water hole was a genuine rock tank where water pouring over the cliffs for centuries has worn out a deep hole perfect for holding water but hard to get at. There were caves in the cliffs above. The only place to camp where there was firewood was several hundred yards away out on the plain; it was a good camp.

Close by was a small tribe of desert Aborigines, who had made their camp fire and bush shelters within sound of our pack saddles. We unpacked water canteens, food boxes, swags, billy cans, bags of flour, sugar, rice and an old canvas sheet that had worn thin with carrying.

Bill did not usually leave the camp either to go hunting for game or to explore the local hills. But this day he chose to visit the native families in their camp.

It was getting time to collect the camels, which wandered away to feed. They were hobbled but I could hear their bells tinkling in the distance, although it could have been a mile away. I decided to bring them back to camp before they got too far away and hobble them out again for the night.

Taking my time I wandered after the bells. In my hand I had an old shotgun. It was fortunate that I had the gun for when I arrived back, the camp had been ransacked. Wade had been visiting the Aborigines' camp, which was at the mouth of the gorge, which meant that anything carried away had to be up the gorge towards the water and the caves, a steep climb with any load. This was the way the thieves had to go for the sides of the gorge were not easily climbed. They could only go up the way of the water hole and there must have been a fair team of strong young bucks to carry the loads. I moved up the gorge, yelling as I went in hope that some fellow would drop his load. I got up past the water to the caves and there was the loot. Only minutes must have elapsed since the carriers had struggled up those slippery slopes with their burden. The problem we now faced was how to protect the precious stores and carry them down over that slope, bit by bit. I was strong in those days, but the job that lay ahead was for me alone.

Bill came for the first load after which he had to keep watch at the camp.

The camels were at risk, too, for a request had already been made that we kill one for meat for the tribe. The situation was one of the worst we experienced in our months of travel in the tribal lands.

When we returned to camp we checked the gear and found not much was missing, mainly a cup.

A year later, and far, far away from the gorge where our goods had been stolen, I attended an old lady of that same tribe who had been badly burned in her camp fire. Glancing at the wooden dishes which are the essential possession of every tribal woman, I chanced to see my aluminium drinking vessel, stolen from that camp in the gorge. It had been one of the very few things we had never recovered.

It so happened that this aluminium drinking pot was the only drinking vessel that I had owned. It was a valued possession out there so far away from the providers of essential things. I had used a wooden pot and a wooden spoon for months after the loss at the gorge in the western ranges. No doubt this humble drinking vessel was a priceless possession for a stone-aged tribal woman. So I left it with the old woman, not indicating that I knew it had been stolen.

Some of the old ones suffered terribly from a disease which eats away the flesh — exactly the same thing as leprosy does. A close relation to leprosy, it is called yaws and it is curable. This affliction, so common to Aborigines in the wild, left me with a feeling of sympathy for those wandering people who had no access to our modern medicine or hospitals. Years later I told Doctor Duguid in Adelaide about what I felt was a terrible affliction among the western tribes. No doubt it helped him to decide to do something for those people — which he did.

It is a commonly held belief that the medicine men of Aboriginal tribes have miracle herbal cures. After my life-long association with Aboriginal people, I can say that this is not quite true. I have seen men with broken legs dragging the unset limb in a pitiful way and men and women with faces or hands eaten away to the bone with the rotting flesh putrid and decaying. There were old ones left to die alone without water or food. This might be the way of the wild, but it is a sad thing to see. Children of the tribes suffer from eye infections that often leave the eye opaque. They have no treatment for bad eyes and often the cure, made by the old medicine men, is to sing the offending body out of a sick man.

Some of the most destructive effects on the Aboriginal people from contact with the whites are the killing diseases, such as measles, for which they have no immunity. When I finally left the ranges, 'Ernabella' became my small contribution to easing my own conscience regarding this.

The one cure, which is as good or better than our medicine, is the poultice made from the ashes of the tchilka bush. For burns it is the best. Also a poultice for infection is a mush made by soaking and heating cactus.

The pituri bush is not a medicine but it is a useful stimulant and it is greatly prized by those tribes who have access to it. This also is mixed with the ashes of the tchilka bush when chewed.

Tribes of those flooded rivers of Queensland had many plants for many ills, but the people who lived in the western deserts did not have the same choice of plants.

The Place Giles Called Paradise

Ten years later: I had seen so much bush suffering that it prompted me to arrange the purchase of 'Ernabella' from Stan Ferguson. Stan had taken a lease at Ernabella Spring after Bill Wade and I told him about the water at that place in the Musgraves.

Doctor Duguid, who was overseas, had left me as convenor of a small committee in Adelaide comprising Murray Care, Miss McCall and Howard Zelling. The money for the purchase was organised by this committee and I, as delegate, arranged with Stan to sell us the lease for five thousand pounds.

When Doctor Duguid came back to Australia we, the committee, were able to hand the lease, through him, to the Presbyterian Church as a medical mission.

'Ernabella' has grown immensely since then. The place is now government run and is the gateway to that vast area which Bill Wade and I explored and which Wade was instrumental in having put aside for the Aboriginal people. Today this immense reserve still stretches through South Australia, the Northern Territory and Western Australia. Coupled with the desert areas surrounding the reserve, the entire area, now available to the Aboriginal tribes stretches over a thousand miles from Oodnadatta at 'Granite Downs' through the Everard Ranges and the Victoria Desert to Laverton in Western Australia.

The next story gives a perspective of the beginning of the missions in the Musgrave and the Warburton area. 'Ernabella' was first mooted when Doctor Duguid called a meeting in the town hall in Adelaide. Someone suggested that a Seventh-Day Adventist mission man from Alice Springs — a camel man with some background of being a bushman — be asked to explore the great central west to see what could be done about establishing a mission there.

Having lately come down from the centre myself, with a child suffering from ophthalmia, I attended the meeting as an invited guest. It irked me to see money wasted on such an exploration when Bill Wade and I had already explored these lands.

Sitting at the back of the hall, I rose and asked the chair (Doctor Duguid) for a chance to speak. Then I told of the years Wade and I had spent in the area under consideration and explained that there was only one water in the eastern Musgraves which would be the gateway to the west, and a mission there would block any whites hunting black women or other interests.

Doctor Duguid asked, 'How could "Ernabella" be got?'

I told of how Stan Ferguson had lately taken up 'Ernabella' as a lease and was living there. Miss McCall rose from the body of the hall and offered a considerable sum of money to assist in the purchase of 'Ernabella'.

After that Duguid was away for a few months. By the time he came back, our committee already had sheep on the 'Ernabella' lease. In time, the Presbyterian Church took it over, then the government as a national project. Since then, the people have thrived.

From here, the question is how does an indigenous group of people make a living and fit into a twentieth-century nation's economy? They certainly could not live only on wallabies, rabbits, and kangaroos, even if they were scattered.

There are now too many people living in a limited economic area, where game is scarce and wheat or rice does not grow. The problem is exactly the same as for Australia's millions of unemployed. Only a strong dictating ruler could take up the reins and put every workable person in the nation, including the Aborigines, to some useful project by finding some work or occupation which would suit them.

There is no lack of work to be done — roads, bridges, reservoirs, land reclamation, essential products to be made here (not imported) — with a balance kept between necessary work for Aborigines and other Australians and funded by an interest-free loan from the Reserve Bank.

Water is the life of the land. If the Glen Ferdinand were damned to conserve a large amount of water, then perhaps rice and corn would feed the people of the Musgraves. Food from water projects is the answer to any nation's basic problem.

The Missions

There is a vast difference between the various missions attempted across Australia. The Derie tribe died out in one lifetime on the Birdsville Track. The German mission at

Kopperamanna was perhaps a noble attempt to Christianise the Aborigines, but with its leader Vogelsang dead, the mission collapsed and the people scattered, their tribal system now destroyed.

The question remains: 'Was that mission good for the Derie tribe?' Very few (if any) pure-bred people of the lower Cooper now survive.

On the other hand, 'Ernabella' mission prospered and still goes well. Perhaps it's because, in those earlier days, Wade had got across his message, as the Aborigines are great singers.

And, note this: No grog was, or is, allowed on 'Ernabella'!

Every year an old rodeo friend, singer Brian Young, goes through the many Aboriginal settlements of the desert areas. Starting in the north-west, he takes a concert party to each isolated community such as 'Docker River', finishing up at 'Ernabella'. From there it has been his custom to ring me wherever I may be to say 'hello'. Some old men at 'Ernabella' still remember Wade and I being there when the tribes were living the old tribal life.

Long after Wade and I had investigated the Everard Ranges, the area was taken up as a cattle station and was called 'Everard Park'. Such desert areas are not very viable as cattle or sheep stations. The whole area, including my old stamping ground 'Granite Downs', is now Aboriginal reserve, adding many, many miles to the western reserves.

In the 1920s, 'Granite Downs' was held as a cattle station covering about five thousand square miles (over three million acres). Those were the days when all the station owners of that area, including 'Mount Chandler', 'Moorilyanna' and 'Wantapella', were living with Aboriginal women and some of them had several. This was the time when the law was passed that those living with tribal women had either to marry them or let them go back to their tribes or tribal husbands. My knowledge of the arrangements was that the husbands of the Aboriginal girls had loaned these girls. Some were certainly bought, while others considered themselves to belong to their white owners.

At that time, about 1928, a few of the Everard and Musgrave ranges' girls had gone back to their tribes. A few were pregnant and some of the half-caste children survived to drift into western stations. A few were taken into missions such as that run by Miss Hyde and Miss Harris at Oodnadatta. The boys and girls, raised and taught by these two fine women, were absorbed into the white community.

As evidence, I was hailed by a group of middle-aged women at Port Augusta in South Australia not so very long ago. They were the children of those station owners who had given up their black wives and sent the children to Miss Hyde to raise.

The Carpenter Bill Wade Talked About

The Carpenter of Nazareth never had a temple. In His time, His walkabout life was akin to that of the Aborigines. Bill Wade preached it that way to the Aborigines, which is as it ought to be.

I myself can feel one with a man of the road, the camp fire and the day-to-day problems of the people. I never could accommodate my own spirit needs with a high priest in high hat and fancy gown before stained-glass windows. It seems to me that, despite the 1900 years or so that preachers have tinkered about with the message, Matthew, Mark, Luke and John wrote about what they remembered.

A change, many changes, have been made to the message. Some say do this or be damned. Some would have us take a dip in water or be sprinkled or be damned. Others insist if we commit a certain sin, which they nominate, we go to hell. I imagine Bill Wade telling the Aborigines about an imaginary hell. A spinifex fire would be the closest they could imagine to hell and those fires were not too bad. They lit them to scare out the game.

The many interpretations of the New Testament never worried Bill Wade. He had accepted the Salvation Army's kind of religion: beat a drum, sing a song. It was a mighty simple creed, definitely out of line with the great denominations. But I am sure it was an acceptable, non-liturgical gospel and Bill was happy with it.

Sometimes the slave in me hated his dogmatic supervision but, in hindsight, the faults were mostly mine. Perhaps the picture I have painted of his mission is too idyllic. Things were not always such.

I remember well the times when a new tribe would be hostile and I thought it advisable to build a shelter from the spearmen who might walk at night. As they did. Selecting a place where young trees grew close together, I would build a circle of thick wall, wide enough to contain a camp fire and two swags, plus the essential cooking gear.

Tracks in the morning showed plainly when we had had visitors in the night. The prowlers would take the straps off the camel saddles and the movable gear would be gone.

We did not go hunting the thieves. It would not have been a prudent move to enter a camp where some of the people were openly hostile. Instead, we handed out a few simple gifts, never mentioning the lost gear.

And Wade soon won them over.

Davey PS 62:1

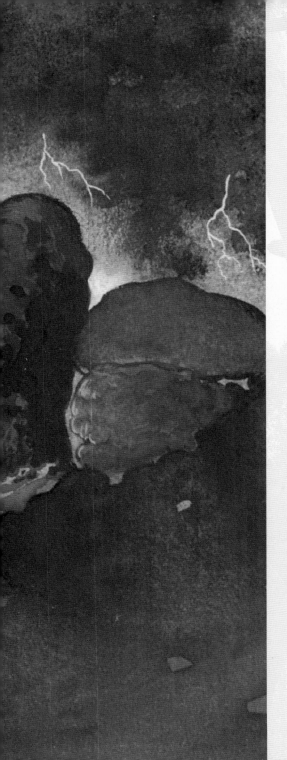

Chapter 12

Journey's End

Give Wade his credit.
It was his crusade.
But looking back,
I somehow feel warmed
by my own small part
in directing history.

Bush Fashions

When a stranger comes into the central Australian cattle country, he is quickly judged by his attitudes, his clothes and his swag (blanket roll). It was cold in the ranges that winter of 1926 when Wade and I had first set out from Oodnadatta. Wade had one of those fancy sleeping bags. It was a known thing in those days that a man was judged by the way in which he rolled his swag. New chums came with the sewn or zipped-up bags.

Men of the cattle camps used open sheets which were so important if the cattle rushed — when seconds meant life or death. Speed to the night horse, which was always kept at the ready, put a man in the saddle to race with or from the mad rush of cattle. A standard canvas sheet was ten feet by eight feet, a size that could make a rain-proof bed in the wet and which folded just right for the iron of the pack saddle.

Camel packs were top-loaded with swags. Top-loading on a camel pack went horizontal. Horse packs required a swag to be rolled right for length and size. Swags on a horse pack doubled over perpendicular and had to fit between the steel hooks. Jumbo swags, too bulky for the width between the pack-saddle hooks, were not for a pack-horse man.

Wade was not a pack-horse man. It seems now what a simple, silly thing that prejudice about bed rolls (swags) was. Nevertheless, these are the ways or fashions by which strangers are assessed everywhere, for did not Shakespeare say long ago, 'The apparel oft proclaims the man.'

Camel outfits included a pair of long boxes made to carry food. These boxes were a source of trouble that never ceased to worry us. Down in the thick mallee country below the Musgrave and Mann ranges, the trees were too close together to let a camel with boxes through. Once we had to go through a narrow pass where the camel could just get through and the boxes had to be carried by hand. Wear, on the corners of the bag loading, constantly caused us to stop for a day and repair the worn corners of the bags.

Every young bushman takes pride in belonging to that elite and so-different clan, 'the stockmen'. It irked me often to see Wade's swag perched so crudely on the pack animals. Fashion did not matter to him as there were no onlookers where we travelled. It has occurred to me that missionaries should adopt the ways of the people among whom they crusade. Tradition among peoples is something that knows no change.

Taking the message of Jesus of Nazareth to a stone-age people who believe in ghosts, is a job for careful thought. Wade was lucky to have a ready-made program in the drum-beating style of the Salvation Army.

Traditions of the past, habits of clothing, styles in saddles, ways of behaviour — all these are products of the generations before us. Boys who follow differing styles and habits were considered strange, even though they may have been innovative and pre-empted change.

This was the case with the introduction of the American saddle, which had its day and was found wanting by the stockmen, who preferred the narrow seat of the lighter Australian-developed style. American long shank bits were not adopted either. Australia had its own saddles, its own bed rolls (swags) and its own clothes, both in cloth and style. These may change, but local traditions do not alter quickly.

The same rules apply to the ways of life, dress and behaviour that the Christian mission insisted on introducing to the Aboriginal people. Women living in the dust of small, earth-floored huts did not have the facilities to keep clothes clean. But the white man's attitude of modesty demanded the Aborigines wear clothes. Sad to say, the changes did not succeed in keeping personal hygiene to a standard of health that the earth-born Aborigines needed. This and their change of diet, together with lack of immunity to imported disease, slowly decimated the tribes.

As I write these lines, the problems of hygiene concerning the northern Aboriginal camps were discussed in today's newspapers — March 5, 1997.

No people could have been more modest than the tribes Bill Wade and I met in 1926–28 in the Musgrave, Mann and Thompson ranges and deserts far out from white influence. They had no clothes and needed none. They had no houses, nor could they have used them, being migratory people. Steel tools they coveted, but stone tools were still in use and, as yet, there were no axes or knives among the peoples of those tribes. Cups were unknown, nor were there any but wooden dishes.

If perchance our own society, so highly developed, were tomorrow flung back to the stone age, every man, woman and child among us would be totally busy just surviving, just making the simple things needed for gathering or growing food.

So many changes have taken place in the past few thousand years. The evidence of the past is there, in the Aboriginal people of my own youth, who were still as basic and primitive as any race at any time.

I bring these people to your notice as evidence that our Aboriginal people of the Australian deserts were still stone-age people in 1926. I met them, lived with them and admired their culture.

In 1928, back in my home base at the rail head at Oodnadatta, a revolution was taking place. The rail to Alice Springs was being built.

It could be said that Mount Margaret, a thousand miles west, had been our home base and later it was again. But, for now, Wade and I treated Oodnadatta in Central Australia as home. Wade had, unbeknown to me, made an alliance with one of the two nursing sisters in the half-caste home. She was Sister Harris who, with Sister Hyde, was feeding and caring for the children of western settlers who no longer wanted to be bothered by their offspring after their black women had gone back to the tribe. Most were like this, but not all. Some white men raised half-caste sons and daughters from their coloured wives and these, as true sons and daughters of the soil, lived on to inherit the land. There are many coloured sons and daughters of the pioneer white men who today are cultured and worthy citizens. Wade later married Sister Harris and took her to the Warburtons.

It might be of historic interest to recount some of the happenings of the years in the settled areas, where we were absent, when the white versus black struggle was taking place.

Passing through 'Granite Downs' in 1928, I had heard the story from Mick O'Donohue about an old dog trapper, Brooks, who had lately been killed by the tribespeople. No doubt he deserved some punishment for his behaviour. But death is so final. The reaction of the settlers at Alice Springs was an expression of the relationship that existed when the law demanded all whites living with black women should marry or return them. This feeling of rejection was expressed in murder. Probably the tribesmen thought the whites had rejected their black women as not good enough.

When Brooks' murder was discovered, the police gathered a posse, rode west and shot every tribesman and woman in sight. The Warrabri tribe were almost eliminated. Those who survived fled east into the Simpson Desert area where it was my lot to meet and work with them in the 'Kurundi' lease and Frew River areas many years later.

At that time the 'Frew', 'Minagi' and 'Kurundi' leases occupied most of the land from Tennant Creek to Hatches Creek and east to the desert border.

The Warrabri were happy there while the head of the tribe, Big Peter, was alive and until the government wrecked his authority by putting the Aborigines in a settlement four hundred miles north under white control. Previous to the killings there had been a good relationship between black and white in the Frew and Kurundi areas.

The Missions

Down on the Finke River the German missionaries, under Pastor Albricht, were doing their best to preserve their relationship with the tribes and they did well. This was a haven for the dispossessed people.

The German attitude to Christian religion was different from the happy drum-beating hallelujah style of Bill Wade, where no demands of cloth or culture intruded into tribal life and where religion depended only on a change of allegiance from witchdoctor domination to an acceptance of 'God as Father'.

I have always believed, and still do, that the garment of a changed heart is better clothing than the dress and trousers demanded by the mission. I learned that the modesty of the naked native women was clothing enough.

Because of tribal boundaries, the Finke Mission run by the Germans had very little connection with the tribes of the western deserts. This, in my opinion, was a good thing.

As I have said, at the mission on the Birdsville Track, the people died out for the simple reason they had no immunity against the diseases of civilisation nor could they adapt to a vitamin-deficient diet of white flour and sugar.

Being given clothes probably had little to do with the drastic change in their lifestyle. But certainly it made no difference to their morality, nor did it make them more adjusted to the new culture.

It has not yet been resolved as to what will happen in the far western deserts of Australia. I hope that there will develop a new nation — changed and adjusted — among the survivors of an invasion for which the tribes had no preparation.

The Women

The circumspect behaviour of tribal Aboriginal women could be explained in several ways. For a woman, any licentious behaviour among her own people meant death. This did not always deter the young girls who fell in love, as many stories of runaway pairs gave evidence. But death, as a penalty, was a major deterrent.

Another custom common to almost all women of Australian tribes was the mutilation of the clitoris, a rough-and-ready operation done with sharp stones. It was a brutal practice, carried out so girls in puberty would not have the same freedom normal to women in our civilised world, except for those Middle-Eastern people who practise the same mutilation of their women.

The total subjection of all females in Aboriginal Australia meant a more demure attitude. Nevertheless, it was evident that those women still living under tribal discipline were modest people of excellent behaviour. Almost always, those girls who were living with white men had been either loaned openly or purchased from a tribal elder — a gesture not understood by European settlers, who mistook this behaviour by the women as promiscuity.

Wandering with Wade

In 1928, after another year of wandering, Wade turned back to the east for essential rations. I had lost all the cutlery, which was not much, but spoons and knives are tools one finds hard to do without. All I had as substitutes were two wooden spoons carved from a mulga bough with my pocket knife. There was no rice or flour. The last ration was salt emu leg. We did get rabbits when we were near the big hills but the rabbits did not seem to thrive in the spinifex desert. There were bilbys there, but these are night animals and are seldom seen in daytime.

Coming in from the west through country where no roads or tracks had yet been pioneered, it was a gamble as to where we would strike a settled area. Wandering, we had lost our exact position, not that it mattered after roaming so long in unlimited desert.

Going east, we knew that somewhere would be the telegraph line from Adelaide to Darwin, which would be a sure guide. The place we first struck belonged to Mick O'Donough, the cattleman we'd met when we first set out, squatting on his five thousand square miles of rough cattle country two hundred miles west of Oodnadatta.

Surprised that the spearmen had not killed us, Mick was pleased to meet us again. He was a man lonely in his kingdom of isolation. We ate well there.

Wade continued east to Oodnadatta. I took the camels and crossed the dry Alberga River to the north towards Queensland, promising to get more camels and meet him again in Oodnadatta. I never did.

My next trip into the Gibson Desert was taken with Gordon Billing, the lad my own age who joined me seeking adventure. We planned to gather dog scalps, of which there were plenty.

Time has erased most of the details of the next year except for the outline of what happened. Wade believed that a strong base such as Mount Margaret, in the northern West Australian goldfields, would be best for him. He selected a place for a permanent mission in the Gibson Desert, which is far west of the Musgrave and Mann ranges. By this time he had married his mission sister at Oodnadatta. No doubt this influenced him to think of a more settled base for his future exploration and his home. He went west to organise camels for the trip, which was planned to start this next time from Mount Margaret.

According to journals available, I had agreed to take camels from Wade's base in Western Australia to find a water and suitable depot in the Warburton Ranges. This did not happen. No doubt I was enamoured of the lure of the unknown, determined to see more of the ranges still unexplored. I regret failing Wade in this agreement.

Taking a few brief jobs to get rations, I turned west again with Gordon Billing, heading for the Great Sandy, as we called the north-western desert. We had heard the rumours that a man called Lasseter had died on a camel trip while trying to find gold in the Petermann Ranges. His story is well known now except, of course, the details of his life with the wandering Aborigines before his death, which was told to me by old tribesmen who were boys in Lasseter's day. Some of these latter experiences of Lasseter are still gossip among the tribe with which he lived.

Preparing another trip into the western deserts was beyond my financial ability at the time of leaving Wade. There was no other way to purchase camels and provisions

but to work for wages and, in the meantime, to collect what dog scalps I could.

This did not take long as I had the opportunity to break in a few camels and my needs were not great.

After Wade had gone back into Oodnadatta and the settled area, I felt the urge to see more of the Gibson and Sandy deserts. Looking back I realise that my motives were in no way inspired by saintly endeavour as were Wade's, who clearly lived and died in the untutored but simple consecration to the Master he had set out to serve. I consider Wade to be one of the saintliest of Christians. In comparison, Billing and I were just adventurous boys.

With Billing, I left the rail head at Oodnadatta, equipped with big stocks of flour, better guns and useful presents for the tribesmen. Wade was to come east from his base in Western Australia. I was to go west from Oodnadatta on the Adelaide–Darwin telegraph line. It is a vast country. Bill Wade and I never met again.

Gordon Billing, inexperienced though he was, made easier company. Often stressed by the exigencies of the road, we never quarrelled. But I missed the never-failing faith of Wade, the untroubled believer.

At the time I really believed that the Aboriginal tribes needed medical help. This was inspired by the traumatic experience of seeing old women and babes left to die when travel became a survival necessity for the rest of the people. When the missions came bringing clothes, they also brought the diseases of civilisation. Settlements lead to government rations; the dole led to drink. The history of this mistake is only seventy years old, but the evidence is plain.

Where with kind intentions the government gathered Aborigines into settlements, the men ceased to learn cattle work and lost the ability to become good stockmen. This has been demonstrated strongly to me in the Frew River area, where fifty years ago the young men were top cattlemen.

Today those same people, nurtured in settlement, cannot or will not behave in the same way.

Who could blame the tribesmen for taking the easy way? They are not to blame. If we had the power of a ruthless Genghis Khan, even a Hitler, we would say:

'This is what the Aborigines do not need. These are the rules by which you will live! For your own good — and yes, for the Aboriginal nation's survival.'

Australia is not like that.

My reason for setting out again and abandoning all social, all personal contacts, was partly to serve Wade's cause, at least that is what I told myself at the time and that is the reason I gave to what small world of people I could call mine.

I wanted to explore, examine and to learn, if possible, about that desert empire of the Aborigines, which the governments of three States later marked on a map (never quite defined) and decreed that only with permission shall a white man intrude. That law still holds.

Give Wade the credit. It was his crusade. But looking back, I somehow feel warmed by my own small part in directing history.

The prime object of Wade's first journeys was to explore in detail the tribal occupation of the three large deserts described in this book. This was done to the best of our ability with slow camels in country where water was scarce and permanent waters very few. The size of the area was too much for our limited time and effort. Nevertheless it has been my experience that, with small exceptions, we contacted some, if not all, of the tribal representatives.

Drawing a map of where I believed we had gone and locating the approximate position of waters, estimating our hours and miles of travel, it seemed to me that the area we covered was large but we didn't cover all the occupied places.

The permanent camp Bill Wade established in the Warburton Ranges, he called a mission. It is now a government-controlled depot and has become, like 'Docker River' and 'Ernabella', a focal gathering point for supplies and service. Wade served out his life there. It can be said that he paid a price in this commitment to the Aborigines.

After Wade

The only predator with which Aborigines shared the game of the deserts was the dog. The yellow dingo was hunted and eaten by the Aborigines, when they could kill that elusive animal. And they trained pups to be hunters for them. Hunted they may have been for centuries, but the dingoes still heavily populated the ranges and the deserts.

It was my intention to finance the expedition with Billing by collecting scalps. When Billing and I told the tribes that we valued the ears of the wild dogs, they could not understand our reason for keeping such things except as a trophy, such as the tip of the tail of the white bilby which the old men attached to their beards as an ornament.

We, of course, knew that the governments of South Australia and Western Australia paid a rich bounty for dingo scalps, for the dingo had multiplied and become a menace to all other game.

The police tolerated missionaries. But Billing and I were an unwanted nuisance. There were only two officers of the law officially responsible for that western area, extending five hundred miles westward from their base at Oodnadatta. Their patrol seldom extended beyond the 'Moorilyanna' water soak, two hundred miles due west of Oodnadatta.

On two occasions rumour reached the police station that cattle killers were coming in from the west as far as 'Tieyan' and 'Granite Downs', the two outer limits of the cattle country. Whether Frank Smith's station, 'Tieyan', had a serious feud with the tribes, I do not know, except that on occasion he had resorted to taking a spearman in chains to the faraway police.

Mick O'Donough would not have bothered. He carried a gun at all times — no one knew whether it was an excuse to go on an exciting primitive mission or because he was under pressure from other cattlemen. Only Virgo, the head police sergeant, would know.

There was only one policeman at Oodnadatta for many years. His arm was long — but whose authority could stretch a thousand empty miles to the west or east and north, even south? It was a big country.

He had fast camels and was feared but seldom seen. In 1928, Gordon Billing and I met him hurrying along, riding the lead camel. His native tracker 'Scoundrel Bob' was riding the fourth camel, and toiling along behind were their prisoners — ten naked Aborigines with steel neckbands, all chained together, with the end of the chain in Bob the Scoundrel's hand. Bob was not averse to giving the chain an occasional tug. They had walked the incredible miles back to trial at Oodnadatta. How do you try a man from the desert whose language was unknown?

The system of neck collars and chains was certainly the only way the elusive tribesmen could have been safely moved long distances on foot. Virgo was a brave man to attempt this hazardous arrest of a group of armed men. And it was a tribute to Scoundrel Bob, the Aboriginal tracker, that Virgo was able to catch a band of elusive tribesmen. I imagine there had to have been a battle, for the spearmen are a very alert people.

The Panic of 1928

Certain tribes were in a ferment. The year was 1928. The Brooks murder by the Warrabri tribe had resulted in many dead following a punitive raid by white settlers, who killed all the Aborigines that they could catch. This is history now.

Men going into the desert had been banned by law from carrying firearms. Word came to us by smoke signals that the pair, Williams and Billing, were to be disarmed — a foolish order to take all firearms from desert travellers.

At the time we passed Virgo and his prisoners, Billing and I were heading into tribal territory. Virgo had his hands full with angry spearmen. He was armed, as were Billing and I, who had no ties. Without a passing word, we walked on. Virgo, the lone policeman, scarcely gave me a passing nod — perhaps? I have often wondered. I know that he would have liked to arrest me, too, but he had his hands more than full.

Weeks passed while Billing and I loitered at 'Granite Downs' with old Mick O'Donough, his brother Tom and a young stockman, Alan Brumby. Alan was a fine horseman who was eager to show his skills. (Just lately — sixty years since I met Alan — three of his descendants have contacted me.)

Tom at the time was a well-sinker. This was before the time of bores in the west. Some of Tom's deep wells were a challenge because of their great depths and inherent dangers. I learned a lot from Tom. In later years he retired from the far north and worked with me making bush gear. (Tom lived with me in Adelaide until he died, years later.)

The law, with fast camels, were on their way to carry out the Virgo edict that Williams and Billing were to be

disarmed. A new young policeman called Francis, set out with Scoundrel Bob the tracker. They believed that their team of five male camels with special police equipment in the way of well-fitting saddles, leather water cans and food boxes made for fast travel, were the best in the north.

Those special leather cans, I envied, and later copied them for storm hunters. In those places, areas were so vast and the air so clear that you could see a storm two hundred miles to the south. Storm hunters would watch those storms, knowing that when the storms passed, there would be grass there for the stock on the desert stations. We would pray those storms in.

By the time Francis set out to find us, no young camel man could have claimed to know more about desert travel than myself. The team of camels I had were desert-broke, feet hardened, gear all tight. Night hobbles had been tested, bell straps were strong, ropes sound.

Billing and I were ready for a chase, and chase it was. Tracks do not erase in the dry areas where the desert crust carries imprints for years. I remember an old bush warrior, Ted Lennon, giving me instructions about how to get to a distant place. He said, 'I went that way two years ago, follow my tracks', and I did.

The policemen of that era were brave men and they were not fools. My respect for Virgo was not awe, but his quiet strength and solemn mien bordered on hero-worship. The young sergeant, Francis, who'd been sent north to help handle the wild men of the gangs building the new line to Alice Springs, was a heavyweight champion of the southern police force. But these fine qualities did not qualify him to chase a trail-hardened desert-wise fellow such as I had become. Although Francis had Scoundrel Bob as his tracker, I knew that tribal boundaries would frighten Bob, and the trackless deserts where sandhills intrude would make his job impossible.

I had seen Francis in action enough not to want to meet him. Perhaps discretion was the name of the game with regard to Mick O'Donough, who was not asked or ordered to surrender his .45 revolver. To take Mick's weapon would have been a death sentence for him, and no doubt others.

So far Mick had led a charmed life, escaping injury on the many times tribesmen had laid in wait for him. His scars were evidence. I understood that while the same enemy had never been around to try again, others took their place. Old Mick had been very polite, even gracious, when Wade had pleaded with him to join the ranks of the saved. Mick never mentioned Wade. Perhaps a hardened old sinner like Mick O'Donough would not have been embarrassed when Wade inquired after the health of his soul.

Billing and I had a good start when the message came through that 'Francis and Bob the tracker are on the way'. Mick gave us salt beef, enough for a long run, weeks if necessary. Which is what it became. West was 'Ernabella', many days' normal travel. This time we did the trip in long non-stop runs, knowing that Scoundrel Bob would go direct as the crow flies.

There was no permanent water between 'Moorilyanna' and 'Ernabella'. The country had not been taken up. After 'Ernabella'. I knew many small waters for the next one thousand miles, it was my country. Scoundrel Bob the tracker had a great disadvantage, he was out of his tribal boundary. A known police stooge, I imagine he would have been a worried man after he had reached the Musgrave Ranges. Wade and I had earlier been friends with the tribes. At least I was known to them and could rely on information about the police who were chasing us. Francis never got closer to us than hundreds of miles.

Billing and I were not outside the law, but we were evading a public dictum issued by the law: to disarm all whites after the terrible massacre west of the Alice. You might wonder why Billing and I were armed. After travelling unarmed with Wade, I had no hesitation in contrasting my insecurity and constant fear of attack with the absolute trust shown by Wade the disciple, the messenger of God, who in complete fearlessness, never doubted his Protector.

I have no reason to believe that my new companion Gordon Billing was afraid. We had not discussed the question. It is sufficient to say that when Billing and I entered the Gibson and Great Sandy deserts we were armed. Strange as it might seem, we were never attacked, as had been previous explorers.

We Meet Giles' Big Men

It is worth noting that Ernest Giles named the creek which he found, The Docker. Now, seventy years after I was there, the Petermann people have been enticed by a need for rations to make this their depot.

Giles mentioned in his diaries the meeting, or rather battle, with the people of 'Docker River' and referred to them as being big men:

> *Two of our new assailants were of commanding stature; being nearly tall enough to make two of Tcitkins. These giants were not however the most forward in the onslaught.*

This bears out the description of men of exceptional height I mentioned meeting in the Deering Hills, about two hundred miles south of 'Docker River'. As Giles met his 'giants' in 1875, they could not be the same men Wade and I met later. Our acquaintances were young men.

Speaking of exceptional men, it might be worth recalling here that there was a tribe of lighter-coloured people to the far north-west of 'Docker River', probably of Malay extraction. The people of that area are definitely lighter in colour than most Aboriginal peoples of the south.

This total freedom of the migrating tribes of the world, including the Aborigines still living in the desert, has some disadvantages, such as no doctors or hospitals. But these amenities, not being known, were not expected. We Europeans are paying a fearful price for our living habits. In fact, it is not beyond possible expectations that taxation might destroy the benefits of civilisation. The Aborigines of the western deserts pay no taxes, no light bills and no rent; they sow no crops and tend no cattle. Their adjustment to the environment is a splendid achievement. Their system of government has lasted for thousands of years, longer than any empire of a more developed society.

Rome is gone, Greece faded, Egypt forgotten. The great empires of Genghis Khan and the kingdoms of China have risen and fallen. But the tribal systems of the Australian Aborigines, so harsh and so ruthless, existed before Caesar and no doubt would have lasted through the great armageddon, or until something like another ice age defeated them. We, the white race, have interfered. Human beings are a fragile people.

One might say, 'But they have no money.' Money is only a symbol of value. The Aborigines have had a barter system for centuries. Their trade routes were sacred to the traders. Goods wanted in the faraway south were supplied by tribes who had ochre, shells, spears, and pituri, the narcotic weed. They were all goods to barter. Money has more substance when the coin is of permanent value such as gold, which has universal exchange value. This we have to relearn after listening to John Maynard Keynes with his fragile paper exchange and the bank of international settlements. The idea that Keynes sold to the world has had its run and, to my mind, failed. We must look again to barter based on gold.

'Primitive' you say! Yes, but it works well for the common people, the masses who have no part in the great banking system that has enslaved most of the world.

Only the Aboriginal tribes and their itinerant brothers scattered around the deserts of the world are free from this enslavement of paper money. Would it matter to the humble rice farmer of China or the wandering Tauregs, or the cattle-minding Ebos, if the civilisation of the West failed. Not at all. They have been self-sufficient for centuries and could remain so. From such as these have conquering nations arisen to defeat Rome, Greece, Egypt.

Foolish, you say, to believe that the unlettered Aborigines might some day become a nation such as the Gauls which defeated Rome.

Seventy years ago, 'Ernabella' was a lonely, unoccupied place. 'Docker River' and twenty such places are now thriving settlements. If you check the number of the children living from Victoria Crossing in the Kimberley to the Nullarbor Plain, and from east to west, you will be amazed at the numbers. The Aboriginal descendants of every city and town are vocal: 'These are our people. These are their lands from time without history. Now is the time to embrace them as one nation black and white. Equal in status, in citizenship, in intellect. NOT as dependants.'

From their ranks are emerging doctors, lawyers, artists. The genes of this people proclaim that they have come from, and are, a nation with a heritage of thoughtful, organised humanity.

It might be said of those tribal people with whom Wade lived that 'they have no learning.' Not true. Their aged councillors carried in their memories the histories of land and happenings of past centuries dating back into the mists of time. The teaching of the young begins at birth. The lore and language of survival, subjects not taught in schools, are the very elements of existence learned by stone-age people, as are the habits of the birds and animals; the seeds of the grasses; seasons that come and go in a rhythm of endless pattern, so necessary to know; the behaviour of individuals and their neighbours, so necessary for survival. All these things are written in the tribal wisdom, tried and proven by centuries of isolated necessity. Were it not for the totem

system developed by observation over centuries, in-breeding would have long since bred idiots who would have perished. The Aborigines of the desert have keen minds which indicate that the totem marriage system has proved to be the best ever.

Among the animals of the world, the strongest ruled the herd and served the females. This was the answer of nature to survival of the race. One looks at the breakdown of any such breeding by selection, or by proven program, and wonders what, if any, chance the new western civilisation has of long-term survival. Our mental problems are increasing, hospitals are crowded — weak bodies and minds are increasing. Look again. Nature has its own answers.

Perhaps because Wade never boasted of himself as a scholar in any way, he must have been that kind of scholar to whom knowledge was an awareness that he had arrived at by devious paths — not by the paths of logic, but by that mysterious intuition some men have.

I have seen him standing alone in the wind or gazing at the stars. After all, does not all knowledge, all wisdom, belong out there with infinity? Sitting by those lonely camp fires, we had heard faint music in the still slight breeze. Was it that music Wade hoped to hear when he seemed to wait in silence alone? Or did he, like Moses or John the Baptist, expect a voice to come? I think he did.

Once a ball of fire came chest-high in an evening camp, disappearing as quickly as it came. The Aborigines listen to these other voices, as well we might, too.

These desert mysteries have stayed with me all through a long life. They are mysteries that knowledge cannot explain and which doubt cannot dispel.

Dreams are mysterious things, but they guide our hands and sometimes shape our lives. The enormity of great distance seems to burst the world wide open, expanding the limited confines of the mind. All of us walk a thin line between sanity and insanity, never quite discerning the great mists of time and space. Few of us accept the responsibility for our actions which, like pebbles in a pool, send ripples the end of which we do not see. Who then can judge Wade, the man, the crusader, the impossible, or even call him a simple man? Perhaps his singular mind, alone with his God, was in fact the great wisdom.

The Old Men

Some, but not all of the old men of the tribe who might be called the medicine men (which is not the right word for them) are the elders. They are the ones who hold the history and secrets of the distant ages, the wise ones, the kind of people we of the new civilisations should let hold the reins of government. These old ones sometimes talked to me of the matters which concerned them. Our lives and material possessions were mysteries to them. Steel knives, cloth, woven bags, leather, buttons, rifles — no such things had been known to them since time began. The making of them was as mysterious to the Aborigines as space travel is to this generation.

Much of what we have and do are very late discoveries. My father would be as much in awe of aeroplanes as the old men of the tribes were in wonder at steel and cloth.

I could use their language a little as time went on, with the result that a few of the old men were willing to talk with me. Even the spirit of communion was a bond between us, for this spirit of good will shone out of Wade like a wave of affection, and some of it rubbed off onto me.

Attitude, attitude. Spirit is everything. It guides, directs and accomplishes.

It might be said that law and order are the prime requisites of civilisation. The Aboriginal tribes of the desert had codes of conduct and laws about every phase of personal, tribal and inter-tribal behaviour. One often hears of the totem or marriage restrictions. This was important as it maintained the nation's physical health, preventing in-breeding. Other laws, which made for obedience to this code, were many and binding. For instance, if a female child was destined at birth to be the wife of the selected husband, often many years her senior, this young woman could not select a young man of her choice. If she dared to fall in love with a young man of her choice, then both might be hunted and killed. Where could an eloping couple go to escape punishment in a land so sparsely inhabited, where smoke signals carried the verdict of the avengers to all tribes. Australia the island was too small for anyone to escape. Aboriginal law was nationwide and binding.

I dedicate this book to the people of 'Yundama', 'Papunya', 'Mount Leibig', 'Kintore', 'Docker River', Warburton, Fregan, Finke, 'Ernabella', and to the many people who have been born there since Wade dedicated his life to securing a place for them:

There are worlds of the spirit where scholars cannot intrude. Wade lived in that world.